"I don't know ho
their names," Ca
a baby onto her hip.

*Two. How was she ever going to manage two of
her own?*

Casey peered down at Stephen, wondering how
any man could look so completely exhausted and
so heart-wrenchingly wonderful.

He'd braced his back against the headboard and
his head was propped against the pillows. His eyes
were closed and his thick lashes swept invitingly
over high cheekbones and a jaw covered with dark
stubble. One of the toddlers had long ago settled
on his lap and lay in the crook of his arm. Another
child used his ankle for a pillow, another his thigh,
while another gripped his strong, callused hand as
if it were a treasured teddy bear.

For some unaccountable reason—or perhaps
because of her own newly aroused mothering
instincts—Casey had the sudden urge to cry.

*What would he say if I told him how lonely I've
been?*

"ABC's," Stephen mumbled sleepily.

"What?"

"ABC's. The girls have been named in alphabetical
 order. Amelia, Beatrice, Cynthia, Darla,
 Eleanor..."

ABOUT THE AUTHOR

Lisa Bingham is a resident of Tremonton, Utah—a rural farming community where the sounds of birds and the rustle of wheat can still be heard on hot summer evenings. She has written both historical and contemporary romances and loves spending time watching her characters grow. When she isn't writing, she spends time with her husband on his three-hundred-acre farm and teaches English at a local middle school.

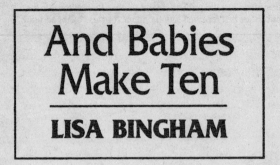

And Babies Make Ten

LISA BINGHAM

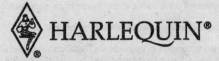

HARLEQUIN®

TORONTO • NEW YORK • LONDON
AMSTERDAM • PARIS • SYDNEY • HAMBURG
STOCKHOLM • ATHENS • TOKYO • MILAN • MADRID
PRAGUE • WARSAW • BUDAPEST • AUCKLAND

ISBN 0-373-16784-9

AND BABIES MAKE TEN

Chapter One

Casey Fairchild pressed her hands to the picture window of the infant specialty shop, Babes in Arms, and fairly drooled at what she saw. Stuffed lambs and bunnies, cradles, rockers, battery-operated swings, car seats...

Never, in all her thirty-five years, had she imagined how the "baby industry" had evolved into such a marvelous display of frippery targeted toward prospective parents—or parent, as the case may be.

Humming softly to herself, Casey yanked herself away from the tempting array, smiling ruefully at the careful placement of the boutique. With a suite of OB-GYNs in the next block, the shop must do a booming business. What expectant mother could resist the sight of ultrasoft blankets, tiny booties and ruffled christening dresses? Even Casey, a pragmatist of the highest order, wasn't immune to such pleasures.

Her lips tipped in a wide grin that had the operator

of a hot dog kiosk glancing over his shoulder to see what had captured her attention.

Unable to control herself, she winked and called out, "I'm pregnant!"

As far as announcements went, on a scale of one to ten, Casey gave herself a "ten." The moment the words were absorbed by the vendor, he blinked in surprise, and a steaming frankfurter slid from the bun he was holding and fell with a splat onto the pavement. A teenage boy fighting to control the leashes of a half-dozen dogs soon found himself dragged to the kiosk. Poodles and schnauzers and an enormous Great Dane besieged the cart as if it were a foreign fort, while condiments flew and a barrage of curses peppered the air.

Quickening her pace, Casey hurried inside the etched glass doors of the Beaman Fertility Clinic. As soon as she'd had a chat with Erica Beaman—her best friend in all the world, *and* her doctor—she would buy something at the boutique as a memento.

But she'd enter the establishment through the rear door, of course.

In case there were any reporters in the area who would love to catch a local radio personality entering such an establishment.

Striding into the elevator, she punched the button for the second floor, then strode into Erica's suite of rooms.

"Is Erica in?" Casey asked the receptionist, leaning over the gleaming mahogany desk, which was more reminiscent of an English study than a physician's waiting room.

The girl eyed her with a strange combination of pity, fear and anticipation.

"She's in her office."

Casey briefly wondered why Erica's current receptionist seemed so much more shy and withdrawn than any Erica had ever had before. But then, she supposed that Erica hadn't had a great deal of input in hiring the girl. Since the Beaman clinic was a family-owned operation—with three generations of Beamans and more than a dozen doctors to their credit—Erica had been offered the services of a distant cousin as her receptionist.

Nearly skipping down the short corridor to the left, Casey tapped once on Erica's door, then let herself in.

"Hey, buddy-buddy," Casey said as she settled into one of the plump wing chairs.

Erica barely seemed to notice her arrival, a phenomenon that had long ago failed to alarm Casey. Erica lived for her work. Even though she had asked Casey to come to her office for a prescription of prenatal vitamins and a chat about her ultrasound, it didn't surprise Casey to see her friend thoughtfully studying the frozen image on her monitor.

"Have a seat," Erica said distractedly.

Casey grinned, noting that Erica seemed even more the "mad professor" than usual that morning. Her dark hair was drawn into its customary chignon, but the knot was slightly askew. Her lab coat was decidedly rumpled, and her fingers drummed the blotter centered on her gleaming antique desk.

Attempting to steer the conversation in the right direction, Casey offered, "I take it you were up all night with deliveries?"

"Hmm."

Sighing, Casey knew Erica was distracted. Accustomed to competing for her friend's attention, Casey slouched in her seat, propping her high-topped sneakers on the stack of magazines positioned behind Erica's phone.

But after several long seconds, Casey noisily cleared her throat. Erica's eccentricities be damned. Casey had less than two hours before she had to be on the air. If she wanted to dash into Babes in Arms, she needed to get going. She had to be back at WMMN for her call-in psychology program at two o'clock.

"Hel-lo," Casey sang out, louder this time.

Erica started, pulling her thoughts back to the matter at hand with obvious reluctance.

"Have a seat."

Casey grimaced. "I *am* sitting."

In an instant, Erica's preoccupation vanished and she turned to Casey, blinking through the lenses of her reading glasses.

"Then maybe you should stand up," Erica said gravely.

Casey's chest tightened with immediate concern. Six months ago, on the eve of her thirty-fifth birthday, Casey had come to a turning point in her life.

Beset with the "blues" and the realization that life was passing by at an alarming rate, she'd listened to a caller at the radio station who had all but parroted Casey's own complaints.

"I'm thirty-five years old and I have yet to find Mr. Right—or even Mr. Maybe, for that matter. All I've ever wanted in life is a child. Instead, I've spent years building a career that doesn't make me happy and looking for a man to 'fulfill me.' I'm beginning to believe the creature doesn't exist."

That moment was still clear and tangible to Casey. Not because the woman had voiced the exact complaints Casey had thought to herself a hundred times, but because, in a flash of insight, Casey had seen an answer to both of their longings.

"So what are you waiting for? We're living in the age of technology. Haven't you heard? Men have become obsolete, at least as a live-in commodity. If you want a baby, if you're totally committed to raising and caring for a child, and you know deep in your heart that a baby isn't some 'toy' to chase away a midlife crisis, then don't let circumstances get in your way. Go find a good OB-GYN and buy yourself some sperm."

Five minutes after recommending such a course of action to a woman known only as Didi in Manhattan, Casey had been on the phone to her own OB-GYN.

Erica had been hesitant about the idea at first, not because of Casey's motives or timings, but because of Casey's medical history. Due to an adolescent bout of ovarian cysts, surgical scarring had made Casey's fallopian tubes all but impassable. Casey's only real option would be in vitro fertilization, a very expensive and time-consuming venture.

Nevertheless, within a month, the process had begun. When the first attempt had failed, it had been Erica who had taken Casey to the movies, plied her with junk food and inane comedies, and encouraged her to try again.

The process had been repeated again and again, until finally, the home pregnancy test Erica had supplied along with a bottle of white sparkling grape juice and a romance novel, had turned a blazing, brilliant blue.

Once she'd confirmed the results in Erica's office, Casey had been ecstatic. But when tests had determined that two of the three embryos had been reabsorbed by the body, she'd been ordered to spend the first trimester in bed in an effort to avoid having the same fate occur to the last embryo.

After three months of daytime game shows and remote broadcasts from her apartment terrace, Casey had held her breath as she'd come for her monthly checkup. She'd known ahead of time that the success rate of in vitro was less than fifty percent with the first procedure, and grew progressively less hopeful with each trial thereafter.

But ten minutes into the examination, Erica had whooped in triumph. The embryo had not been reabsorbed. It was still hale, hearty and growing more each day.

So why did she appear so concerned now...?

"Is something wrong?" Casey breathed, barely able to form the words, feeling her rosy outlook for the future shift around her as she mentally scrambled to brace herself for the worst.

Erica's laughter was so genuine that Casey felt a slight easing of the fist clutching her heart.

"Don't be so dramatic." Erica's brows lifted. Sliding her reading glasses down, she peered at Casey over the rims. "Even though, with you wearing that getup, no one could ever think you'd act otherwise."

"What's wrong with my...getup?" Casey said, glancing down at her red high-tops, purple overalls and lime green shirt.

"Nothing. It goes great with the hair. You look like an elf on Prozac."

Casey grinned, fluffing the short, pixielike cut she'd adopted. With her spiky mahogany locks and her indigo eyes, Casey realized that Erica's wasn't the first reference she'd received to the Little People.

Catching sight of the monitor screen behind Erica, Casey immediately sobered. "Is that my ultrasound?"

"Yes."

She focused on the dusting of white spots over gray over black, but for the life of her, the still picture looked more like a Rorschach test than evidence of life.

"So what's the problem?"

"That depends on how you look at things." Erica

pushed her glasses into their proper position and reached for the remote, pushing the play button.

Immediately, the Rorschach test came to life, and as the grainy spots began to shift and slide, Casey's gaze was drawn to the center of the screen. There lay a tiny, pulsing mass.

"Is that...?" Her hand reflexively dropped to her stomach as she dropped her feet to the floor and leaned forward.

"You're still very much pregnant," Erica confirmed.

"Then why scare me like you've been doing?"

"You don't understand." Erica took a pen from her drawer and, using it as a pointer, motioned to the side of the delicate embryo. "Casey," she offered slowly, "you are *very* much pregnant."

Casey blinked, regarded her friend, then the monitor. Finally, she saw what Erica was referring to. Slightly behind and to the right of the embryo was another separate pulsating blob of gray and white.

"Twins?" Casey whispered in disbelief, her mouth growing so dry the word barely emerged.

"Congratulations."

"Oh, m'gosh," she groaned in disbelief, her stomach flip-flopping with nerves and agitation.

Twins.

A baby...she'd been ready for a baby. *A* baby. One. *Uno.*

Of course, multiple births had always been a possibility with the in vitro process, but when only one of the embryos had escaped being reabsorbed, Casey had thought that possibility was beyond consideration.

"I thought that the other two eggs were reabsorbed."

Erica shrugged. "Evidently, we were wrong. Either that, or nature may have had its own plans."

"Plans?" Casey echoed, still stunned.

"The cells may have divided naturally. The twins could be identical rather than fraternal."

"Identical." The room seemed to grow fuzzy around her.

Erica smiled as she flipped off the monitor and stood. She stripped off her lab coat, hung it on a hook on her inner door, then swung the portal wide to reveal a spacious bathroom decorated in delicate pinks and mauve.

"Wow." The word was more of a sigh than an exclamation. Standing, Casey slid her hands in her pockets and studied her toes. Twins. Two babies. *Two*. Two cribs, two potty chairs, double strollers…

Her stomach twisted, then lurched.

"Oh, m'gosh. Twins!"

Then, amid Erica's accompanying laughter, she raced into the proffered rest room as morning sickness reasserted its ugly head.

"YOU CAN'T GO BACK TO WORK."

"I *have* to go back to work. I've got…*twins* to support."

"You are also over thirty, single, with a high-risk pregnancy. You've got to slow down."

Casey groaned, dropping her head on the shiny bar of the Juice Joint—juice being the closest thing she'd been able to find to a good bracing shot of brandy. Unfortunately the guava-banana-orange combination that had become her favorite comfort food over the past three months was not having the same effect as a jolt of liquor. But she had to think of the baby.

No. *Babies.*

"We'll all end up in the poorhouse," she mumbled morosely. "My babies will be dressed in rags." Her voice choked in misery. "I'll have to keep them in a…in a…drawer."

Erica's snicker didn't help in the least.

"Buck up, old buddy. I've already taken matters into my own hands."

Casey lifted her head up enough to stare at her friend. "How?"

"I got you a job."

"I have a job."

"You'll have to take medical leave from the radio station."

"Why?"

Erica sighed. "We've been through that already. Your job at the radio station is a high-pressure, high-profile, high-stress situation that—as your doctor and your friend—I can not allow you to continue."

"But I gotta eat," Casey said as she reached for the jelly bean dish on the counter. When Erica deftly switched the candy for unsalted, unbuttered popcorn, she grimaced. So far, morning sickness had not been an overwhelming problem. The nausea usually made an appearance when she was upset, overly tired…or delivered a stunning piece of news. In fact, her appetite was the most astounding part of her pregnancy to date. She was continually famished, her cravings running the gamut of expensive Swiss chocolate to junk food.

"You'll eat. I promise. Plus, you'll have a part-time job, room and board, and a quiet familial neighborhood where everyone takes care of everyone else."

Casey eyed her friend, knowing that this time Erica had lost her mind. Such places didn't exist outside the realms of fantasy. "Where is this mythical land? Oz?"

She took a sip of her juice.

"No. Kansas."

Casey choked and reared back, spattering her T-shirt and overalls with juice. "You've got to be kidding. You're sending me to Kansas to have this— these babies?"

"It will do you good. I've got a distant cousin there who—"

Casey closed her eyes. "Not another Beaman physician."

"No, actually, this cousin is from my mother's side of the family—I think he's fourth or fifth removed and—"

"Just get to the point."

"He's a pastor."

"That sounds jolly," Casey groused as she blotted the juice from her favorite pair of overalls.

"Hear me out. The man is a pastor in one of those small towns—you know, the kind where everyone knows everyone else."

"It sounds like Mayberry."

"That's about right from what I understand. Anyway, he's been looking for someone to serve as his part-time assistant."

"Doing what?"

"Helping in his office, arranging flowers for the chapel, some light secretarial duties."

Casey still wasn't mollified. "So why hasn't anyone in Mayberry snapped up this dream job?"

"Because he's looking for someone with a psychology degree who can also help him to organize some local support groups."

"What kinds of groups?"

"The usual."

Casey's eyes narrowed. Why was the hair on her neck beginning to lift in suspicion? Usually, such a phenomenon was saved for Erica's mother when she tried to fix her up with some "nice young man who was down on his matrimonial luck."

"What kinds of groups?" she repeated.

"Marriage counseling, Al-Anon, you know the sort."

"Like I said before, why hasn't somebody already snapped up this dream job?"

"Because the pay is lousy, the hours are irregular, the room and board supplied are in the rectory, and the town is forty miles from a city large enough for a McDonald's. All of which led me to the conclusion

that the whole setup was tailor-made for you...
Mama.''

Casey's mouth was already open for a pithy retort
when Erica's last word stopped her cold.

Mama.

Of twins.

Closing her eyes, she pressed the heels of her
hands against her brows to help her think.

She was thirty-five years old, pregnant, and on the
verge of a major life change. Moreover, as Erica had
explained, she had been placed in the "high risk"
category of expectant mothers due to her age, occupation and the nature of her pregnancy. So how could
she refuse the advice of her physician and long-time
friend when Casey knew everything Erica had said
was right?

The next few months were going to be stressful
enough. Why complicate matters with the demands
of her job? Especially since her outrageous sense of
style, blunt advice and rollicking personal appear-
ances had drawn her into the limelight more than she
had ever thought possible. As soon as the tabloids
and gossip columns caught wind of her pregnancy...

She didn't even want to think about the possibilities. She could already see the headlines.

Shock-Doc Takes Her Own Advice!

"Talk a Lot" Host an Unwed Mother!

Doc Fairchild Is Single, Pregnant and Loving It!

Suddenly, Kansas looked like heaven. The thought
of working for a kindly, middle-aged man of the

cloth brought with it images of peaceful nights, farm-yard chats and sunsets.

"When can I start?" Casey said resignedly as she lifted her head.

Erica grinned. "I'll get on the phone with my mother as soon as we've finished lunch. I'm sure she'll have all the details and a phone number we can call to clinch the deal."

CASEY SQUINTED in the gathering gloom of the late-spring evening, then glanced at the hand-drawn map Erica's mother had provided her.

"Less than ten days after I discover there are two of you, here we are. Ruckerville, Kansas," Casey shouted to her tummy as she drove.

The noise of her vintage Super Beetle and the Mozart blaring from the tape deck caused a passing farmer in his tractor to stare at her as if she were the strangest sight he'd ever seen.

Grimacing, Casey supposed she would have to tone down her personality over the next few months. No doubt she made an odd sight—a woman talking to herself driving around in an ancient car that defied the sound barrier. But she'd grown accustomed to talking to her babies—a practice that all of her research books had encouraged. And even though classical music was about as high on her list as a root canal, the Mozart was beginning to grow on her. Mozart, she'd read in one book, was supposed to be good for brain development. How, she didn't know, but she was willing to take a pair of Harvard Ph.D.s at their word.

Glancing at the map again, Casey frowned when Erica's warnings of this being a *small,* small town had not been exaggerated in any sense of the word. So far, just about all she'd seen was a glorious landscape of farmland. Isolated houses with neat yards sat amid plowed fields sprouting with what looked like rows and rows of tender grass, but which she had been informed was new grain. In the distance, she could see the town, and she was sure she could throw a rock from one end to the other.

Well, nearly.

Slowing her Beetle to the prescribed twenty miles an hour, she counted two gas stations, a battered movie house, a drugstore, grocery store, bank, post office and hardware store—all of the buildings looking like something out of a B-grade movie, complete with tall, narrow facades proclaiming the original construction dates and titles of the edifices.

Easing to a stop at the only traffic light she'd seen in twenty miles, Casey patiently waited for it to change, even though there wasn't a sign of another car in miles.

"Quaint. Very quaint," she shouted to her twins.

A woman stepping from the corner drugstore started in surprise, hurriedly latched her door and strode in the direction of the flat brick post office.

Chagrined, Casey adjusted the volume and drummed her fingers on the wheel.

"This is an incredibly long light for such a little

place,'' she mumbled. "Maybe it's timed for creeping tractors.''

Sighing, she leaned forward, peering around Al's Fuel and the Maverick Movie House to her left, looking for a spire or bell tower to help her find the church. According to her map, she was to turn west—if and when the light changed to green—and drive until she saw the church. If she reached the railroad tracks or the manure pit of the fertilizer factory, she'd gone too far.

Casey's nose wrinkled at that tidbit of information. Somehow, she feared manure and morning sickness could prove a lethal combination, and she'd prefer to avoid such a place at all costs.

Sighing, she began to fidget.

"This is absurd,'' she muttered, glaring at the light.

Miraculously, the red flickered, disappeared, and the green lamp blazed into the night.

"Hallelujah,'' Casey whispered under her breath. But before she could ease off the clutch and gun the engine, the green light vanished, the yellow light flickered, and the red lamp blared its warning.

Swearing, Casey stamped on the brake, killing the engine in the process.

Cursing under her breath—so the twins wouldn't hear—she started the engine again, growing more and more self-conscious with each minute that passed. In the block ahead of her, she could see the doors of the fire station swing open. To her delight—astonishment, horror, pleasure?—a group of tanned, half-naked, sweat-slick, muscle-bound men raced into the night.

Judging by the banging of the basketballs against the sidewalk and the good-natured banter, some sort of tournament had just finished and the winning team and its fans were being teased and challenged by their opponents.

Shrinking into the shadows of her car, Casey prayed no one had seen her stall the Beetle, even as she wondered at the sight. Here was small-town living at its finest. A drugstore with a single lock and no alarm system. A one-light intersection, damned slow though it might be. City-league basketball, a firehouse gym, and country folk who actually enjoyed interacting with one another.

Erica was right. This was exactly what Casey needed. The peace of nature, the slow bustle of a small town, the grace of country living, and a pastor who could serve as a grandfatherly role model.

Perfect. Just perfect.

There wasn't a thing more that she could ask for, except…

Casey's thoughts stalled as abruptly as the Beetle, when a solitary figure turned away from the gaggle of people moving toward parked pickups and minivans. Alone, he came in Casey's direction, causing her mouth to grow dry.

One side effect that Casey hadn't counted on in her pregnancy was a heightened sense of sensuality. The appreciation of silk and velvet, long candlelit bubble baths, and men.

Athletic men.

Muscular men.

Perspiration-slick, lean-featured, drop-dead gorgeous…men.

Her limbs began to tremble as he hit the corner curb, then crossed diagonally to her car. As her headlights fanned over well-formed calves and thighs, slim hips, an even tighter, harder waist, and a broad chest coated with a loose, cut-up T-shirt, her stomach flip-flopped in a very pleasurable way.

He stopped at her window, bracing a forearm on the roof of her car. The other was looped around a scuffed basketball. Leaning down, he offered her a glimpse of razor-sharp features and short black hair that curled damply against his scalp.

"Can I help you?"

Casey tried her best to speak, but the sound that emerged from her throat was a croaky gasp.

"You're new around here," the man commented in an obvious effort to put her at ease.

"How'd you know?" she finally managed to whisper.

"New York license plates, the I Love Manhattan bumper sticker and the U-Haul trailer were dead giveaways."

She laughed, but the noise was more of an embarrassed croak.

"Don't worry. Even in an unmarked car, you would have given yourself away."

"Oh?" Dammit, why had she lost her ability to speak?

"This intersection…" he said as he shifted to rest the crooked arm with the ball in her window frame. "That light hasn't worked in years. Anyone local treats it as a four-way stop."

Casey gasped, then glared at the light for putting her in this awkward position. Talking to a stranger. A handsome stranger. A virile stranger.

An I've-got-to-get-out-of-here-before-I-totally-lose-the-rest-of-my-dignity stranger.

"C-can you direct me to the church, please?"

"Sure."

To her astonishment, he didn't speak, but rounded the Volkswagen and opened the passenger door. Picking up her briefcase and the leftover sack of munchies she'd placed there for her trip, he folded himself in the passenger seat.

Casey fought to breathe normally when she felt the space had been completely invaded with long legs, bare skin and sweat-dampened athletic attire.

"I'm headed that way," he said as he lobbed his ball into a back seat stacked with luggage.

"Y-you live near the church?" she asked as casually as she could, half praying he did and half praying he didn't.

He chuckled, a throaty, rumbling noise that began low in his chest and made his eyes crinkle in fun.

"Very near," he offered with a wink. "I'm the pastor."

Chapter Two

Stephen Dubois watched in amusement as the woman's features grew pale, causing the freckles spattered over the bridge of her nose to become even more evident.

"You're the pastor?" she whispered.

Stephen chuckled. He was used to such a reaction from those who were new to his small parish. He'd learned long ago that most people expected a man of the cloth to be middle-aged, somewhat paunchy and dry as dust.

"I am," he whispered, leaning close as if confiding a secret. "But don't tell anyone."

He offered her another trademark wink—one that the elderly women in his congregation described as cheeky and the teenagers thought was "too cool."

But rather than encouraging the woman, the gesture merely seemed to fluster her even more.

"Th-then you live at the…"

"Rectory?" he supplied helpfully, watching with

something akin to fascination as her indigo eyes became faceted with specks of gold.

"W-which is next to the..."

"Church."

"Oh, my G—" She bit back the rest of her statement, biting her lip.

Stephen laughed at her expression of horror.

"It's not that bad. Honest. I'll take you there without incident. I won't bite. Really."

Her gaze skittered away from his, and she blinked up at the red light.

"You can go ahead anytime you're ready," Stephen prompted.

Again, she stared at him with wide eyes. Gold-and-indigo eyes. Incredibly expressive eyes. In their depths he could clearly read confusion, fear and a touch of something very much like...wonder?

"I think ten minutes of waiting can be considered a full stop," he said, but his brain wasn't centered entirely on the traffic light. Something about this woman's frank regard was pulling at him, demanding his complete attention—as if he might miss something wonderful if he looked away.

He wondered what could have brought such a woman to Ruckerville.

And how long would she stay?

She wrenched her attention back to the light and put the car in gear. But as she accelerated, her opposite foot slid from the clutch and the car lurched, then stalled in the middle of the intersection.

She swore under her breath, then flushed an even brighter shade of red. "Forgive me, Father."

He laughed. "I'm not Catholic."

Her cheeks blazed.

"People around here usually call me Stephen."

She shook her head. "I couldn't."

"Why not?"

She pulled a face. A cute, alarmingly intriguing face. One that made his gut tighten in a curious and completely worldly way.

"It's so…informal. I—I mean if we're going to be…"

Going to be…

As he waited for her to finish her statement, he firmly kept his brain from finishing the phrase with his own unlikely list of words.

Friends?

Very good friends?

Very, very good friends?

"Working together."

She spoke again, and the conclusion of her previously uttered sentence skittered over his subconscious like a rock over a glassy pool. Then, *plunk,* the meaning of her reply sank into his head and the whole situation became incredibly clear.

Glancing at the contents stuffed into the back of the car, he noted the boxes, luggage and a fish bowl wedged into the space behind her seat.

"*You're* Casey Fairchild?" he asked, even as his body began to debate whether this woman's identity was about to become a gift or a temptation.

"Yes."

Her admission was little more than a puff of air.

He studied her again, taking in her spiky hair and the outrageous orange T-shirt and loose, flowered, summer-weight jumper she wore.

He laughed again. "And here I've always prided myself on being a man of the nineties."

Her brow furrowed in confusion.

"I thought Casey Fairchild was a man," he explained ruefully.

Again, she looked as if the world might crash around her feet, so he waved the comment aside with a sweep of his hand. "But that's neither here nor there. In fact, I think that your being one of the gentler sex will be the best thing for the support groups you'll be forming. Somehow, I always feared how the single mothers would confide in a man. Two of them are in their late teens, unmarried and pregnant—horribly confused."

At his words, she seemed to weave a little in her seat.

"Father?"

"Stephen," he reminded her.

"Do you think you could drive us to the church? I'm afraid I'm not feeing very well. Not well at all."

STEPHEN DELIVERED HIS NEW employee to the rectory in record time. Retrieving the gold fish bowl, his ball, and her overstuffed purse from the back, he told her he'd help her unpack later. Then he ushered Casey inside, deposited the items on the counter, and handed her a glass of water, but she refused to hear of his calling the town physician.

"No. I'm fine. Really. I've just been on the road too long."

Leaning against the counter, he crossed his ankles, surveying the woman who was about to become his assistant.

"By the looks of you, I'd say it's been a while since you've eaten a good meal, too."

She blinked at him with those gold-and-indigo eyes.

"What makes you say that?"

"You look like a ghost."

She grimaced. "I have naturally pale skin. Even a month in the Caribbean couldn't give me a speck of color." She made another adorable face. "Other than red. I've been known to imitate lobsters on occasion."

He opened his mouth to tell her that he'd already seen several delightful shades of pink touch her cheeks, but quickly reconsidered.

"How about some supper?"

"Supper?"

"Yeah. You know, food."

Her grin was so sudden, he found himself smiling in return.

"I really must be in the Midwest. I don't think I've ever heard anyone use *supper* in a sentence."

"Then you've been associating with the wrong people," he said, his voice emerging in a gruff tone that unnerved him.

Settle down, Dubois, he cautioned himself as he moved to the refrigerator. *This is your assistant—and a psychologist to boot. You have no business thinking of her as anything but a member of your congregation.*

Even though he was very much single.

And the supervisory board would like nothing more than to see a quick end to his bachelor status.

"Stephen, is that you?" a quavering voice bellowed from the adjacent hall, and for the first time in minutes, Stephen relaxed.

Ahh. A chaperone.

"In here," he shouted.

Casey was obviously startled at the volume of the exchange, so he quickly explained.

"I don't live alone at the rectory. The previous pastor passed on about four years ago. His widow and her two siblings live here with me." He dropped his voice to a whisper. "They're all a bit deaf, but Grandma Myrtle is the worst."

"Then why are you whispering?" Casey asked, her own voice church-quiet.

Stephen laughed. "Force of habit, I guess."

Grandma Myrtle shuffled into the room, then paused in the doorway, her rheumy eyes immediately settling on the newcomer.

"Who's she?"

"That's Casey Fairchild. My new assistant."

"What?"

"Ca-sey Fair-child. My...*assistant!*" Stephen shouted. Obviously, Grandma Myrtle had left her hearing aid near the television again. She refused to use the "new-fangled contraptions" that had been custom-fit only a month earlier. Instead, she wore the same Kennedy-era amplifier and earpiece she'd used for the last forty years. Invariably, she would sit down to watch her programs, set the amplifier on the side table, then leave it, earpiece dangling, when she went to the kitchen for a snack.

"What?"

Stephen set some eggs and cheese on the counter and helped Myrtle onto one of the chrome-and-vinyl chairs.

The entire dining room set looked as if it had been stolen from a fifties malt shop, and Myrtle had to brace her feet—clad in their perky bunny slippers—against the floor to keep from sliding off.

"She's my assistant," Stephen yelled into her ear.

"Then she shouldn't be going out in the rain, should she," Myrtle primly snapped.

Stephen was used to the way Myrtle mysteriously interpreted whatever she'd heard. But when he opened his mouth to explain the phenomenon to Casey, she drained her glass of water and said, "I get the picture. She couldn't hear an atomic bomb detonate next door."

"Exactly." Stephen gestured toward the back room. "I'll just go get her hearing aid."

"What?" Myrtle called.

"I'll get your hearing aid!" Stephen shouted.

"What?"

He patted her shoulder to calm her, then pointed

to his ear and the general direction of the television room.

"That's right," Myrtle said with a decisive nod. "You'd better give her a call right now. She said it was an emergency. A *dire* emergency."

Stephen grew still. "Who called, Myrtle?"

"I told Anne we should have gone to get you, but she wouldn't hear of it."

"Myrtle...*who called?*"

Myrtle patted him in the general direction of his rear.

"Then why don't you take a shower and change into something more suitable for your date."

Stephen opened his mouth, thought better of shouting questions, then offered Casey a helpless shrug. "I've got to go unravel this mystery. Make yourself comfortable, Casey. I'll be right back."

As Casey watched Stephen Dubois disappear into the rectory, she exhaled, willing the tension to ease from her body just as easily.

That was the pastor of this idyllic little town? *That* was her employer?

Shaking her head, she wondered what sort of game Erica was playing to set her down in the middle of this...this...

This *what?* Nothing had happened here.

Well...nearly nothing. So what if learning her boss was a handsome, athletic, virile, exciting *young* man had set her off balance? Even if Erica had met Stephen Dubois, how was she to know that Casey would react to him as if he were…were…

A Chippendales dancer?

"Stop it," she whispered to herself.

"What?"

The old woman was peering at Casey as if she'd grown another head.

"Stephen was going to fix us something to eat."

"What?"

Needing to do something—anything—that might divert the old woman from staring at her, Casey gestured to the food on the counter. "Maybe I should take over. I'm not a fantastic cook, mind you, but I can fry an egg. Want one?"

There was no answer.

Sighing, Casey said, "So have you heard the news? I've just been made the assistant to a very attractive man, one who definitely kicks my libido into high gear. But, wouldn't you know it? I can't indulge in any lascivious thinking because A, he's a pastor, and B, I'm about to become the mother of twins."

"What?"

Casey rolled her eyes. "Never mind. You sit there and pretend to listen, and I'll talk and cook us all something to eat. Deal?"

"That's what I told him. An emergency."

"I'll take that as a yes," Casey muttered under her breath as she reached for the eggs and a block of cheese.

STEPHEN FOUND ANNE and Bert in the television room. The elderly woman—who made eighty-year-old Myrtle look like a young girl—had tuned the channel to pro-wrestling while Bert dozed in his recliner.

"Do any of you know anything about—"

"On your desk," Anne interrupted, then returned to jeering Pretty Boy Freud's performance with the fluency of a stevedore.

Snapping off dozens of lights as he went, Stephen made his way to his office. Somehow, none of his elderly companions managed to turn off a light when they left a room. Perhaps it was an unconscious response to surviving lean Depression and blackout war years. He'd have to ask the new psychologist.

Casey.

Pushing the image of the lithe young woman ensconced in his kitchen out of his head, he hurried to his desk and shuffled through the pink message slips until he located one with Emergency scrawled across the top.

Stephen didn't immediately recognize the number other than to determine it was preceded by a foreign area code. But the moment he noted the name of his foster sister, he sank into a chair, his adrenaline levels returning to normal.

Lexi Polanski had come to live with Stephen and his mother when Stephen was little more than a boy. She'd stayed with them for five years—a record for Lexi, who admitted she was a free spirit with itchy feet. At eighteen, she'd joined the Peace Corps, and she'd been traveling ever since. The last he'd heard, she'd been in India, studying Hinduism. Before that, she'd played in Malaysia, and before that a rock band in Brazil.

Dialing the number, Stephen drummed his fingers on the blotter, listening to the clicks and snaps of an overseas connection. Finally, amid a cacophony of static and what sounded like a fife-and-bugle corps massacring a rendition of "Hey, Jude," he heard a garbled "Alo?"

"Yes, I was given this number—"

"Alo?"

"Do you speak English?"

"Alo?"

He tried again, this time in French. *"Parlez-vouz—"*

"Stephen...is that you?" another voice interrupted.

"Lexi, I can hardly hear you."

"What?"

Stephen closed his eyes and rubbed the spot at the bridge of his nose, which was beginning to ache. He had a feeling this phone connection was going to make talking to Lexi as easy as a conversation with Myrtle on nuclear physics.

"Lexi," he shouted into the mouthpiece. "Myrtle said there was an emergency."

"Yes...in a hurry...my flight...Samoa..."

"Samoa? You're *in* Samoa? Or you're heading to Samoa?"

"In Western Samoa...actually...hot..."

This time, it was Stephen's turn to cry "what?"

"Delivery…you will."

"What?"

"Fa…ther of…all…"

"Lexi, you're breaking up. What are you saying?"

"Will you…please?"

Even through the static, Stephen could hear the note of panic in her voice. "Lexi, I'll do anything you need. You know that. Just tell me—"

"Thank, you, St…tha…you…thank…you…"

Then the line went dead.

Stephen frowned, wondering what he had just been thanked in advance for doing. Groaning—since favors for Lexi often bordered on the outrageous—he redialed the number. But a tinny voice informed him, "All circuits are currently busy. Please try again later."

Leaning back in his chair, Stephen closed his eyes. Just one moment. One moment of silence, of serenity, of peace. Then he'd drag his sorry butt out of the chair and make himself useful.

"Bad news?"

He jerked, wondering how long he'd been alone— or asleep—when he found Casey Fairchild standing in front of him. She carried a battered silver tray that held two plates with steaming omelets, a tall glass of milk and a cup of coffee.

Embarrassed, he wiped a hand over his face.

"Was I asleep?"

"Just dozing."

"Sorry."

"Don't be. You couldn't have been unconscious for more than ten minutes."

"That sounds like more than mere dozing."

She set the tray on the blotter, her expression mischievous. "Will I be fired in advance for lying to a priest?"

"Pastor."

"Whatever."

He took the proffered plate and fork, wondering when he'd smelled anything so delicious. "I take it you aren't a…"

"Religious zealot?" she supplied when he searched for a diplomatic description.

"I don't think the term *zealot* even entered my mind."

Shrugging, she dragged one of the heavy antique chairs to the opposite corner of the desk. The chair nearly swallowed her whole as she sank into the battered leather tufting.

Completely unselfconscious, she folded her legs beneath her, then grabbed her plate and the milk.

"I went to church as a kid."

"Which one?"

She appeared to be searching her memory. "Let's see…my earliest memories are Episcopalian, Methodist, Catholic and Lutheran. My elementary years were Baptist, my junior high years Buddhist, born-again Christian and paleontology."

Stephen had been taking a sip of coffee, and he choked. "Paleontology?" he spluttered.

"Just checking to see if you were listening—although my mother did attempt to make it a religion of sorts.''

''I see.''

She laughed, continuing to eat her omelet with the enthusiasm of a true gourmand.

''I can assure you that you don't. My parents were what most folk would call hippies. Free love and free knowledge. They were at Woodstock, you know. I believe it was the first concert I attended, although I couldn't have been very old. My little sister was conceived there. She's a faith healer in New Mexico—lives in a hogan.''

Stephen had been about to drink again. Deciding the eggs might be safer until this topic of conversation was finished, he set his cup on the tray.

''But then again, I suppose that's more than you need—or want—to know. Suffice it to say that a good deal of my life revolved around a townhouse in Greenwich Village and an outrageously painted Volkswagen bus.''

Carefully chewing his omelet, Stephen decided that the food and the company were the best he'd had in ages.

''Is that what made you become a psychologist?''

She thought for a moment. ''I don't think so. Frankly, I'm a naturally nosy person, and it was the only way I could transform such a quality into a career.''

Again, he laughed, and as he did so, he felt the stress of an active—and somewhat hellish—day drain away.

"So what made you consider taking a job as a pastor's assistant in Ruckerville, Kansas?"

Her eyes narrowed, and he thought for an instant that a shadow crossed her features as she debated her answer. But when she responded, it was with the same flippant tone he'd come to expect from her.

"I've seen Oz, I thought I'd try Kansas."

He knew there was something more to her reasoning than a whim to see the Midwest, but he didn't pry. He'd obtained Casey's services through a distant cousin—and he'd already been ordered to see that Casey ate right and had plenty of rest since a recent surgical procedure had left her needing the time and space to recuperate. Since most of his Beaman relatives were physicians in one way or another, he hadn't asked for details other than a reassurance that her condition wasn't catching, her treatment was finished, and she merely required rest.

"This is great," he said, pointing to the remains of his omelet with a fork.

"Thanks. I guess that's one advantage of being a hippie love child. I can scrounge up a decent meal from whatever odds and ends I can find."

Stephen's fork hung suspended halfway to his mouth. The term *love child* seemed to hang around his head like an invisible cloud.

Forcing himself to complete the movement, chew and swallow, he wondered how long it would take to become accustomed to Casey's candid—and oftentimes outrageous—replies.

"How long have you been a psychologist?"

"Twelve years."

His brows rose. She didn't look much more than twenty-three or four. Surely he didn't have a child genius on his hands. His congregation would be gossiping enough at the fact that he had announced *Mr.* Casey Fairchild's impending arrival. Once they got a good look at the beautiful woman he'd mistaken for a man, tongues would be wagging in glee.

"How old are you?" he asked without preamble.

She pretended to look shocked. "Don't you know that it's impolite to ask a lady's age?"

She fluttered a hand in front of her face as if growing faint, and he found himself entranced. Casey had known him less than an hour, but her banter was as playful as if they'd been lifelong friends.

Or lovers.

He quickly banished the thought.

But he wasn't quick enough to catch the fork that slipped through his fingers and clattered onto his empty plate.

Chapter Three

As the clang of silver against china reverberated in the room, Stephen winced. The woman sitting opposite the desk looked far too amused for Stephen's own comfort.

"What's the matter, Stephen? Are you worried that you've hired someone barely beyond the age of consent?"

"The thought did cross my mind," he admitted reluctantly.

Again, her expression grew wicked. "Hmm. I wonder what Freud would say about that?"

Before he could answer, she stood and began to stack their plates on the tray.

"But you can rest easy. I'm thirty-five—and I have the driver's license and the crow's-feet to prove it."

Crow's-feet? Was she kidding? The tiny lines that fanned from her eyes had nothing to do with age. Instead, they proclaimed that she was a woman who laughed often and well.

"Let me take that," he said as she lifted the tray.

"You will not. You're the father, I'm the assistant—remember?"

"I'm not a father, I'm...never mind."

He forcibly removed the tray from her hands. "This is your first night, and though I am madly in need of an assistant, I wouldn't dream of asking you to fetch and carry for me. That isn't why I hired you."

Her eyes held his for a moment too long, the golden flecks deepening.

"What if I insist?"

There was a feather-light edge to her tone that caused the muscles of his gut to tighten. Reminding himself that this woman was here for some sort of recuperation, he determinedly stepped past her and into the hall.

"Try to resist insisting," he muttered.

She fell into step behind him. "Why? Are you stubborn? Or merely a control freak?"

He shot her a glance over his shoulder. "You're already psychoanalyzing me?"

"That's what most people expect of me on the first encounter."

"Well, I don't."

"You don't what? Expect me to analyze you? Or want me to analyze you?"

"Both. Either. Neither. Hell, I don't know."

She snickered under her breath at his soft curse, but thankfully, he was saved from a response by the ringing of the phone.

Sighing, he handed the tray to Casey. "Do you mind?"

"I already volunteered."

"Yeah. Right."

Retracing his steps to his office, he grabbed the portable phone, then, suddenly conscious of his attire, he yelled, "I'll be out in a minute, Casey. I've got to take a shower and change before I show you your quarters."

He heard a muffled response, then Myrtle's "What did he say?"

Tucking the phone against his ear, Stephen took the stairs two at a time. "Rectory, Fa—Pastor Dubois speaking."

"Etienne, this is your mother," a harried voice announced on the other end. Katie Dubois had a habit of announcing herself, even though he invariably recognized her voice. She also invariably used the French version of his name whenever she was upset or in a hurry.

"Hi, Mom. What's up?"

"I just got off the phone with your brother."

Stephen rolled his eyes as he stepped into his quarters—a sitting room, bedroom and adjoining bath reserved for his own use.

"Mom, I already know about Jean-Luc's new position."

Stephen's parents had met and married in Vietnam while his mother had served in the army. Two children had been born from the union and were given impossibly French names despite their dual French and American citizenship. Ten years later, the couple had split up. Jean-Luc had been raised by their father, Etienne by their mother—a very confusing arrangement that had resulted in one son becoming a priest, and the other a pastor. It was while Stephen was in the seminary that he'd adopted the Americanized version of his name. He'd discovered Etienne Dubois was too much of a mouthful for most Midwestern Americans.

"This isn't about his new posting—although how playing basketball with those street kids is supposed to save souls, I don't know."

"He's organizing an intercity league, Mom."

"Whatever. That's not why I called. Frankly, Jean-Luc and I have been trying to reach you for most of the evening."

Which would probably account for the rest of the pink message slips that Stephen had forgotten to examine.

"I had a call from Lexi."

"Yeah, I just—"

"A horrible connection. I couldn't make out a word."

"Mom, I talked to—"

"Evidently, she also called your brother in New Orleans."

"I—"

"She was sobbing and crying and carrying on."

Stephen gave up trying to insert any information he'd gathered himself. When Katie Dubois had a bee in her bonnet, it was best to let her "vent."

"Jean-Luc couldn't make heads or tails of the whole story, so he called me. Of course, I had no idea that she was in Samoa—"

"Western Samoa—"

"Whatever—until I managed to get in touch with Cousin Sally in Orange County. She had me call Stella, who told me that Granny Weston had received a letter only last week."

Closing his eyes, Stephen sank onto the edge of the bed, trying his best to keep track of the relatives involved.

"Anyhoo, Granny Weston laid a bomb, I can tell you that much."

"What sort of bomb, Mom?"

Stephen rubbed the bridge of his nose again. Lexi was good for at least one or two outrageous antics a year. Katie Dubois and every relative within phoning distance would work themselves into a frenzy of gossip and wonder, then settle down again until the next flare-up.

"Father Dubois?"

The call floated to him from downstairs. *Father* Dubois. Maybe he should call Jean-Luc and have him explain the difference to Casey Fairchild.

"Yeah?" he called, covering the receiver.

"There's someone at the door. He'll only talk to you."

"I'll be right down. Tell him to wait in the parlor."

"You're sure?"

"Yes."

"Okay." There was an if-that's-the-way-you-want-it note to his assistant's voice.

"Look, Mom, I—"

Wondering how much longer this day would last, Stephen dragged himself into the bathroom.

His mother was still talking. "Married. I would have sent a—"

"Mom, hold that thought for just a second. I've got to put you on hold."

Depressing the appropriate button, Stephen showered quickly—deciding it was probably just as well that the water emerged with a bracing chill.

In less than two minutes, he was back on the phone and toweling off.

"Go ahead."

His mother picked up exactly where she left off. "Gift… After all, Lexi is my daughter. I've said so a thousand times. I would have dropped everything to attend the wedding—"

"Wedding?" Stephen interrupted as he slid into a pair of well-worn jeans. "Lexi is married?"

Katie Dubois groaned. "Haven't you heard a word I've said?"

"Father Dubois?" Casey's voice was accompanied by footsteps on the stairs, and Stephen hurriedly zipped his pants and reached for a sweatshirt.

"Mom, when did Lexi get married?"

"Nearly two years ago."

"And she didn't invite us? She didn't even tell us?"

"Etienne Philip Dubois, are your ears painted on? That's what I've been telling you since you called."

"But, Mom, *you* called."

"A point that is neither here nor there. The fact is that Lexi got tangled up with some guru type in India and now she's frantic since the marriage is over."

"Father Dubois?"

Stephen froze, his arms threaded through his sleeves, his chest bare, the drops of water cold against his skin as Casey burst through his door, then hesitated, her eyes latching onto his chest.

"Mom, I've got to go."

"Etienne, I haven't even got to the reason I called!"

"I'll call you right back. But I've got to go."

Before his mother could protest, he punched the button to end the call, dragged the sweatshirt over his torso, then ran his fingers through his hair. Through it all, he was overtly aware of the crackling energy that filled his rooms and made him completely conscious of the woman who watched every move.

"There's…uh… I think you'd better come downstairs."

Vaguely remembering that he'd told Casey to usher his unknown guest into the parlor to wait, he forced himself to move. Brushing past her, he ignored the velvety friction of skin against skin as their arms met.

"Welcome to the life of a pastor," he muttered as he hurried down the staircase and into the parlor.

Since Myrtle had rejoined her siblings, the volume to the television had been increased to a deafening level.

Stephen grimaced as he thought of his foster sister. What in heaven's name was going on with her?

And what had he promised to do?

"Yes," Stephen barked in the direction of the unfamiliar man, his voice emerging much more abruptly than he'd meant it to.

The stranger, who was all but buried in the sagging wing chair, jumped to his feet, exposing an express-delivery service uniform and a clipboard.

He snapped to attention, his hand lifting in a half-formed salute before he caught himself and extended the clipboard instead.

"Sign, please."

"Why?"

The man rolled his eyes. "I have a delivery for a Pastor Stephen Dubois. Are you Stephen Dubois?" His scathing regard of Stephen's casual attire and the blaring television left Stephen in little doubt that the man was skeptical about such an assertion.

"Yes. I'm Stephen Dubois."

"Sign, please."

"But I didn't order—"

"It's not an order, it's a delivery," the gaunt, sallow-faced man reasserted—as if such a statement explained everything.

Surrendering to the inevitable, Stephen signed the appropriate line. Next to his name, he saw the name Polanski and the package's origin, New Delhi.

So this unexpected surprise was Lexi's doing. Maybe he wouldn't have to attempt another overseas call to discover what she needed.

"Leave it on the porch," Stephen said as the man from Speedy Delivery made his way through a sea of recliners and elderly wrestling enthusiasts.

The man's lips pursed in disapproval, but he didn't complain.

Stephen navigated the room in the opposite direction, finally managing to reach the television. He turned the volume down to a tolerable level, then located Myrtle's amplifier and adjusted it to its maximum setting.

"I think you'll find this more comfortable, Myrtle."

"What?"

Sighing, Stephen wearily made his way to the porch.

The deliveryman had already deposited a large object in the shadows of the porch and was making his way back to his van.

"Thanks," Stephen called, then, hearing a creak in the hall, motioned to Casey. "Will you flip on the light? It's the one to the far right."

He was just closing the distance to the package when the wraparound porch was flooded with a glaring yellow light. Blinking his eyes to adjust to the two-hundred-watt bug bulbs that Anne had installed in the overhead lamps, he frowned.

Lexi had sent him a chair. A very small chair. A...

When the blankets he'd assumed had been heaped

on the seat moved to expose a tiny fist, then a chubby cheek, he closed his eyes and began to pray in earnest.

If his muddled senses were to be believed, Lexi Polanski had just sent him a baby.

And he had a horrible feeling he'd just promised to take care of it.

"WOW," CASEY MURMURED as Stephen carried the car seat into the rectory and closed the door with his foot. "I didn't know you could send kids next-day air."

She watched as Stephen's face displayed a gamut of emotions from panic to resignation to wonder.

"Is it yours?"

He shot her a pithy glance. "No. I told you I was single."

"Gee. Last I heard, being single wasn't the best form of birth control."

His jaw dropped, and he shot a warning glance at the wrestling fanatics.

"I'm a pastor," he explained under his breath. "Abstinence is one of the job requirements."

Casey knew she was being completely "fresh," as Myrtle had accused in the kitchen when Casey had added a dash of hot sauce to Myrtle's omelet without asking first. But Casey had learned long ago that life was not meant to be bland.

Which was probably why she now found herself as the assistant to a pastor.

In the background, Myrtle shouted, "Beat his head into the mat! Crush him to a bloody pulp!"

Casey blinked, cleared her throat, then gestured to the child. "Who does the baby belong to, then?"

He checked the tags dangling from the carrier. "My foster sister, evidently."

The insistent ringing of the doorbell urged Casey to answer it so that Stephen could remain with his...

Foster niece?

But when the door swung wide, it was to find the deliveryman on the threshold, his mouth twisted into a painful grimace of disapproval. At his feet was another car seat, another bundle of blankets.

Another pink fist.

"Oh, Stephen," she called as she hefted the car seat into her arms and closed the door with her foot.

Stephen appeared in the threshold, making Casey feel incredibly small.

His mouth dropped when he saw what she carried. "You've got to be kidding."

"This is not my doing, remember?"

He took the car seat from her arms and disappeared just as the doorbell rang again.

Wondering if the town grapevine was even more remarkable than she'd been told, Casey opened the door.

But it wasn't some nosy member of the congregation who'd come to check out the latest addition to the rectory. It was the deliveryman—Stan, according to the patch on his shirt.

"Another one?" she asked in amazement, taking the car seat from the man as he staggered.

He rolled his eyes, but was huffing too hard to answer. When he looped the diaper bag he'd been carrying over Casey's shoulder, she could see why. The thing weighed a ton.

"I'll be back," the man wheezed. "I've got two more to go."

"Two more babies?" Stephen asked in disbelief from the doorway.

"Yes, sir."

"Stephen?"

She had to give the pastor credit for his response. Although he grew pale and cursed under his breath, he remained relatively calm. He grabbed the car seat and helped the deliveryman bring the other babies indoors.

"I didn't think pastors were supposed to curse," she remarked as she followed him into the parlor and gratefully dropped the diaper bag on the floor.

"I'm a pastor, not a saint."

She regarded the five sleeping toddlers. She wasn't an expert on children, but she'd place their ages somewhere between two and three. "Someone obviously thinks you're some kind of martyr."

The doorbell pealed again.

"Blast it all, Stephen, can't you hold that racket down?" an elderly voice shouted. "We're trying to watch television in here."

Groaning, Stephen muttered, "What more could the deliveryman want?"

"A bi-i-ig tip," Casey remarked, turning on her toe.

Stephen returned seconds later. This time, he carried a cage with a fluffy, lop-eared white rabbit.

By this time, even the wrestling fanatics had abandoned the spectacle on the television to stare in amazement at the drama unfolding in their own home.

"What is *that?*" Myrtle shouted, her tone no less strident though she wore her amplifier.

"They're children, Myrtle," the balding, stoopshouldered Bert replied.

"No kidding. But what is that animal?"

"A rabbit," Anne said with a sniff, crossing her arms in disapproval. "I don't think it's proper for such an animal to be in the house. It's loaded with germs."

The deliveryman shook his head and backed toward the door. "Take my word for it and don't move the thing outside."

Then he beat a hasty retreat to the door.

"Hey, I owe you a tip or something," Stephen said, following the man.

"No. No, that's fine. Just sign this release and I'll take my leave. I've accompanied these girls since Kansas City when they were left in my care by a pair of missionaries."

The man all but ran to the van, gunned the engine and sped into the night.

"Well, I don't care what the mailman says, that

animal is going outside," Anne grumbled as she grasped the handle and marched to the door.

As if some sort of incantation had been spoken, one pair of baby eyes opened, then another, and another, until all five sets were wide and wondering. As if they were used to traveling en masse, the toddlers seemed to take stock of their companions, ensuring that no one was missing. Then a cloud of doubt settled over the group. Shifting, kicking, stretching, they tugged at their restraints—timidly at first, then more and more determinedly.

"What's wrong with them?" Myrtle barked.

"Isn't it obvious?" Anne said with a scowl. "They want to be let loose."

"You make them sound like a herd of cows," Bert said forlornly.

Of the group, Casey was beginning to take a shine to Bert. He seemed to be the only adult other than Casey who appeared sympathetic with the children's plight.

"Poor things," she murmured. "They've probably been in those seats for hours."

She knelt to grapple with the buckle of the car seat closest to her, but the baby pushed at her with frantic hands, obviously searching for something other than her siblings.

One toddler began to cry, the others falling suit until the din was tremendous.

"What's wrong with them?" Anne cried impatiently, her lips pursing in disapproval.

Myrtle wrenched her earpiece free and stuck a finger in its place.

Searching frantically, Bert snatched a pair of doilies from the arms of the couch and began to play peekaboo.

Stephen knelt on the floor and did his best to release one of the youngsters. But the wriggling, squirming body would not allow him to help her.

"Do something!" Bert said in alarm, abandoning his antics, his hands wringing in empathetic anguish. "They're hurt. That deliveryman must have drugged them to keep them quiet!"

Casey surveyed the scene before her, taking in the desolate children and the alarmed adults.

"I wonder..." she murmured.

But no one heard her.

Turning on her toe, she hurried back to the stoop, retrieved the rabbit cage and brought it back to the parlor, setting it on the floor in front of the quintuplets.

The quiet was so sudden that Stephen lost his balance and sat on the floor, his hands draped over his knees.

Myrtle exhaled in relief.

Bert clapped his hands. "There's a girl with a good head on her shoulders, pastor! You'd better keep her around."

Even Anne's lips twitched in approval.

"I suppose this means the rabbit will be living indoors," Stephen said with a lopsided smile.

"So these…children are here to stay?" Anne inquired.

"So it would seem."

It wasn't clear what Anne thought of the idea—and Casey doubted that Myrtle had heard the statement since she was bending over the cage, poking her cane through the holes to ensure the placid rabbit was alive and not some toy.

Bert, however, was overjoyed. "How marvelous!"

"Where are we going to put them?" Anne asked stiffly.

"We've got plenty of room."

Stephen rolled to crouch in front of the nearest car seat again. Now that the child was calmly sucking her thumb and staring at him through tear-filled eyes, he was able to unhook her easily enough and move on to the next baby.

"All of the rooms are in the guest wing, not the pastor's quarters," Anne informed him.

"I'm sure we can arrange some cots or something in my sitting room."

After a few minutes, the children were free. Timidly at first, they crawled from their seats, revealing that they'd been dressed in identical ruffled overalls, but each child had been distinguished with a different shade of T-shirt.

Standing, Stephen planted his hands on his hips. As he surveyed the gaggle of babies who grew braver and began to roam the room, it became evident that he was still a trifle shell-shocked by the sudden change of events.

"So when does the next deliveryman appear with their mother?" Casey asked.

He grimaced. "I have a feeling that she's not coming."

Casey's lips formed a round O, but she didn't speak.

Stephen gestured to the babies with a wave of his hand. "This must have been the 'emergency' phone call I missed. When I tried to call Lexi back, I couldn't understand what she was saying because of the static. She said something about a favor..."

"Some favor." Casey eyed the five toddlers—all girls, she would assume from their feminine attire and headbands. Instinctively, her hand touched her stomach, and she wondered if her own babies would be little girls she could dress in ruffles and bows.

"So what are you going to do with them?" she finally asked, her voice husky from her own inner ramblings.

"I have absolutely no idea."

It became evident that the toddlers were overjoyed at being free and allowed to roam, because as soon as they realized the adults were not about to shoo them into their car seats again, they began to run—faltering, unsteady steps at first, from one end of the room to the other.

Then, the bravest of the children—one with a blazing red T-shirt—squealed in delight and made her escape from the parlor, running as fast as her little legs could go.

In an instant, the other girls followed suit, scattering in different directions—the stairs, the corridor, the kitchen.

Casey stared in amazement, wondering how such tiny beings could move so quickly.

A crash came from one of the distant rooms, spurring Stephen into action.

"I'll take the office, you take the stairs. Bert, the kitchen, Myrtle the hall…"

"What?"

Anne harrumphed and returned to her spot on the couch before she could be assigned a room.

Giggling, Casey hurried in the direction of a pair of imps crawling up the staircase. From all around her, the house seemed to come alive with thumps and squeals and babyish chatter.

Stephen was only halfway to his office when the doorbell rang again and he froze.

Even Casey felt a twinge of anxiety.

Not another set of babies. How much was one man supposed to handle?

But the "yoo-hoo" that floated through the open windows did not belong to Stan the deliveryman. The tone was very high, quavering and demanding.

Stephen's eyes squeezed shut and he raked his fingers through his hair.

"Trouble?" Casey asked, grabbing one squirming toddler and carrying the child down to the ground floor.

Stephen grimaced, an expression of near horror crossing his features.

"You could say that," he said, each word filled

with dread. "That's Nola Wilkens. Our nearest neighbor and president of the Ruckerville Ladies' Aid Society."

He took a deep breath, squeezed Casey's shoulder and offered, "Brace yourself."

Chapter Four

Casey stretched, breathing deeply of the cool morning air and luxuriating in crisp sheets that smelled of sunshine. She couldn't remember the last time she'd ever slept so completely. So wonderfully.

There really must be some truth to country life being food for the soul, she thought as she pushed the covers aside and swung her feet to the floor. As she yawned and rubbed her eyes, she conceded that it had been years since she'd felt so relaxed and rested first thing in the morning. Erica had been right to send her to Ruckerville, Kansas.

Even though Casey's best friend couldn't have envisioned that she would be sending Casey from her own frenetic world to one that had grown just as chaotic overnight.

Laughing to herself, Casey stood and rummaged through the suitcase that she'd placed on the floor at the foot of the old iron bedstead. Locating the fish food, she offered her pet some breakfast.

Sometime between one and two in the morning,

she'd been ushered to the east wing—a portion of the rectory that dated back to the late nineteenth century. As Anne had shown her the amenities—a bathroom down the long hallway with a seven-foot-long claw-foot tub and brass radiators, and her own tiny bedroom with an antique standing wardrobe and dresser—Casey had been informed that the rectory had once doubled as a school. The east wing had four double-occupancy rooms, which had once housed teachers and visiting officials, as well as two large student dormitories. For nearly one hundred years, this section of the church had been used as living quarters by children from some of the outlying areas who boarded at the rectory during the week, then returned to their homes on the weekends.

Casey laughed softly to herself as she remembered the way Anne had pointed out the rooms she and Myrtle used along the same corridor. The tone she'd used had made it obvious that she and her sister weren't there for company so much as to prevent Casey from falling into mischief. Then, to underscore her point, the older woman had used a large skeleton key that hung around her neck to lock the double doors that led into the main portion of the rectory where the pastor and her brother slept.

"These doors are always locked at night. Always," Anne had said, infusing her voice with the same importance she might use when informing a pleb of the location of the Holy Grail. But even now, Casey wasn't sure if the locked door was to keep her *in* or the males out.

In any event, after meeting with the Ladies' Aid Society president, Nola Wilkens, Casey supposed that she should be grateful to Anne for ensuring that the minister's house would not be tainted by scandal. From the moment Casey had been introduced, Nola Wilkens had all but vibrated with disapproval. Over and over again, she'd made it clear that the pastor had informed them that a *Mr.* Fairchild would be arriving. Clearly, the mistake was Casey's, and she should do everyone a favor and change her sex or leave.

When it became evident that Stephen had no intention of booting Casey out the door, Nola Wilkens's thin lips pursed into nothingness. From that moment on, the woman's barely veiled comments made it clear that the Ruckerville mamas were going to be less than thrilled about having another young single woman to contend for the pastor's attention.

Casey grimaced, wondering what Nola's reaction would have been if Casey had blithely informed her that the entire situation was much more dire than the president of the Ladies' Aid Society had supposed. Not only was Casey single, but she was pregnant, irreverent…

And more than half attracted to the pastor, despite the woman's warnings.

The moment the thought jumped to the fore, Casey banished it. She was *not* interested in the pastor in any way other than as her employer. Heaven only knew that she had enough complications in her life right now. She didn't need to add a man to them.

Let alone a man who'd recently been entrusted with the care of quintuplets.

As she hurriedly changed into a pair of drawstring pants, a tank top and an oversize cotton shirt, Casey winced as she wondered how the pastor had fared with the toddlers. The last time she'd seen the tribe of five, Bert had been helping to shepherd them in the general direction of Stephen's quarters. But judging from their squeals and spontaneous dashes for freedom, the nap they'd had during their travels had completely recharged their inner batteries.

Tiptoeing over the creaky floorboards, Casey made her way to the locked door. She was hoping that Anne had already awakened. If not, she wasn't quite sure how she intended to escape. Slipping through a second-floor window held no real appeal, but neither did the thought of being trapped in her room until she was summoned.

"Good morning, Miss Fairchild."

Casey jumped at the voice from behind. Glancing over her shoulder, she found Anne standing in the doorway of her own room. Her iron-gray hair had been savagely combed into finger waves against her scalp, and she wore a neat rayon dress with a cotton sweater thrown over her shoulders.

"Good morning, Miss...Anne."

Nearly colorless eyes blinked at Casey as Anne fastened a bejeweled sweater holder to either side of the knitted plackets. Casey wasn't sure, but she thought the pincers on either end of the elaborate chain were fashioned in the shape of claws.

"Are you ready to assume your duties this morning?"

"Yes, ma'am," Casey obediently replied. She resisted the urge to shift from foot to foot like a guilty schoolgirl, but there was something about the dormitory setting and Anne's piercing gaze that reminded Casey of her brief stint in parochial school. Casey was probably overreacting, but she was sure that Anne's stern scowl mirrored the same disapproval Sister Mary Simon had displayed when the nun had caught Casey smoking in the bushes. At the time, Casey had been seven years old, and Sister Mary Simon had not been amused.

"How did you sleep?"

"Very well, thank you."

"It's the lavender."

The comment was uttered so matter-of-factly, Casey wondered if she'd somehow missed an obvious point.

"Lavender?" she asked as Anne's orthopedic oxfords thumped across the hardwood floors.

"The laundry. I rinse the linens in a concoction of my own design before hanging them out to dry. Lavender is the principal ingredient."

Casey blinked. That had to be one of the most wonderful rituals she'd ever heard of. On those days when Casey ran out of clean clothes and was forced to do the wash, she was lucky to remember fabric softener, let alone a special rinse cycle laden with aromatic herbs. Amazed, she wondered if Anne's pragmatic facade was merely camouflage for a true romantic.

Anne unlocked the double doors and opened them wide for Casey. As the elderly woman's scowl deepened, Casey shook away such nonsense. Anne a romantic? Impossible.

The moment Casey had stepped into the adjoining corridor, Anne snapped the doors shut, then made her way to the landing.

"Follow me, please," she ordered. "You may wait for the pastor in the kitchen."

Casey had already planned to do just that, but something about the woman's pronouncement inspired the oddest urge to break away, run to the west wing and do something "naughty."

One look at her companion stilled the impulse.

Anne's eyes narrowed as if she'd read Casey's thoughts. And in that moment, Casey knew that Anne would do everything in her power to ensure the pastor's virtue remained untainted—even if it meant tackling his assistant in the hall.

Remembering Anne's enthusiasm for wrestling, Casey folded her hands together and fell into step behind her escort.

"Should I talk to Ste...the pastor about getting my own key?" Casey asked as she dutifully trotted after the tall, stern woman.

"We'll see."

Anne's reply had the same note of doubt an adult might give to a child wanting ice cream for breakfast. It was obvious that Anne might allow Casey to live in the rectory for the time being, but she didn't necessarily intend to trust her.

Since Casey had yet to be told about her official duties and the hours involved, she trailed Anne all the way to the kitchen. With any luck, Stephen would already be there and Casey would be liberated.

But the room was empty.

"I—I'll just go check and see if St…the pastor is already in his office."

"He won't be," Anne informed her tartly.

"Well…I'll just check."

Unfortunately, Anne's prediction proved to be correct. Stephen's desk was scattered with the same phone messages as the night before, and there was no evidence that anyone had been in the room since then.

For heaven's sake. Where was the man? Was Casey doomed to be dogged the rest of the morning by an octogenarian chaperone?

Sighing, she returned to the kitchen, knowing she was doomed to wait for the minister to make his appearance. Until he did, she couldn't wander through the rectory in search of something official to do. Anne would definitely disapprove of such a course of action.

"Your food is ready," Anne said when Casey returned.

"You didn't have to make anything for me. I—"

"It's my duty. I will not shirk my duty."

Casey opened her mouth, then shut it again. There was no suitable response to such a comment.

Throughout the sparse breakfast of black coffee, one slice of bacon, one piece of dry toast and one tablespoon of jam, Casey prayed that the smells would draw her employer out of hiding. But she and Anne had finished eating, washed, dried and replaced the dishes they'd used, without a sign of the man.

Donning a pair of gardening gloves, Anne left the kitchen without so much as a goodbye, and Casey was suddenly alone and completely at a loss as to what to do. She'd fully expected Anne to shadow her steps until the minister appeared.

So why did the woman's sudden abandonment make her feel...wicked? Impulsive.

Hearing a faint murmur of conversation, Casey followed the noise to the parlor, where she discovered Myrtle instructing Bert on how best to rearrange the contents of the bookshelf so that the breakables would be above toddler level.

Bert offered her a cheery "Hello, little lady!"

Myrtle merely stared.

"Have either of you seen Stephen?" Casey finally asked.

Myrtle squinted and shouted, "What?"

"Stephen. Have you seen Stephen?"

"It's in the refrigerator next to the eggs."

Bert snickered. "She's left her hearing aid upstairs again."

"What?"

"I said you're deaf as a post, woman!"

"Thank you. It's new."

Stifling her own chuckle, Casey threw Bert a quick wave. "Thanks, anyway."

Returning to the main entry, Casey slid her hands into her pockets and rocked back and forth on her heels.

She had only one more possible place to look. But after the frowns of disapproval she'd already received from Anne and Nola Wilkens, she wasn't sure if she would be destined for the pits of hell if she dared to make her way to Stephen's quarters. Surely such behavior would be far too shocking.

Of course, she'd been there before.

And the minister had been bare-chested and beautiful.

A bolt of sexual energy shot through her body, and she shivered in reaction.

Damn, these hormones were making life so…so…

Interesting. Almost as interesting as a broad-shouldered, water-dappled man of the cloth—without the cloth.

"Stop it!" Casey whispered under her breath. She'd already been inundated by the popular opinion that she was a lustful woman out to bag the minister as some sort of sexual trophy. Did she have to prove to everyone that Anne and Nola were right? That it was impossible for a young, single woman to serve as an assistant to a young, single minister without sex getting in the way?

Sex. With a minister?

That wasn't allowed, was it?

Not that you would—or could—indulge in such a liaison.

Thankfully, before the little devil whispering in Casey's ear could pursue the thought much further, Casey heard a thump from the direction of the second floor, then padding footsteps. Tiny, furtive, childish footsteps.

The children. Of course. If Casey really felt it necessary to have an airtight excuse for wandering into the "forbidden zone," she could always blame her behavior on the quintuplets.

Nevertheless, she still felt the overwhelming need to creep through the house like a thief, clinging to the shadows against the wall until she was out of sight of anyone who might make a sudden appearance at the bottom of the staircase.

As she moved down the hallway, the noises grew louder. Rustling, baby jabbering, bumps and thumps.

And a curse. A very masculine, sleepy, grumpy curse.

Emboldened by Stephen's mutterings, Casey straightened. Noting that his door had been left ajar, she eased it open—praying she wouldn't find her new employer in a state of dishabille....

And half hoping she would.

But when Casey caught her first sight of the minister's quarters, she gasped.

What on earth had happened here?

Makeshift sleeping arrangements had been made by dragging mattresses from the east wing and setting them on the floor. But it was obvious that the quintuplets had spent very little time sleeping. The room was a shambles of rumpled bedclothes, diapers, bottles, open drawers, broken furniture, mangled sports equipment, and rabbit paraphernalia.

"My gosh! Was it a tornado or an earthquake?"

Dark, tousled hair and a rugged masculine face appeared from behind the bed. Casey's jaw dropped when she saw that the minister's weary features were liberally streaked with red-and-blue stripes of what appeared to be war paint.

"Who drafted you?" she asked with a grin. "The Comanche or the Apache?"

"Shh!" Stephen quickly hissed, then added more softly, "Don't make a noise—no noise!"

"Fine," she whispered, clearly noting the panic and frustration in the warning. Judging by the reaction, spending the night with the toddlers had been less than a picnic.

Padding into the room, Casey rounded the antique tester bed. There, she discovered two little bodies curled next to Stephen on the floor. Judging by their poses of abandonment, they were deeply asleep.

"You finally wore a pair of them out, I see," Casey commented with a smile.

"The rest of them escaped into the bathroom. See if you can catch them before they decide to try flushing another of my sneakers down the toilet."

Casey choked back the instinctive laughter that rose in her throat.

"What's with the war paint?" she asked as she tiptoed past him.

"Hell if I know. It amused them for about an hour."

She paused in her travels long enough to say, "Is your congregation aware of the vocabulary you employ when you are under extreme duress?"

Stephen was clearly not amused. "I've had ten minutes of sleep all night. In the past nine hours, I've watched a five-woman demolition crew dismantle my living quarters and most of my belongings. I've read *Good Night, Little Rabbit* at least a hundred and sixty times, been pushed, poked, prodded and drooled on. Frankly, I think my language is exemplary."

A flushing noise caused Casey to rush into the bathroom, where next to the toilet she found the same red-shirted imp who had led the charge for freedom the night before. Her sisters were hovering next to the shower. Just as Stephen had predicted, one toddler was in the midst of attempting to flush a shoe down the toilet. Unfortunately, this time the footwear in question was a dressy leather oxford. Probably something the minister wore on Sundays or special occasions.

"Hands up!"

The child started, dropped the shoe on the floor, but kept one finger on the flushing lever—making Casey wonder what else could be floating in the bowl.

"Back away from the toilet..." Casey paused, then whispered into the bedroom, "Do you have names for any of these children?"

"Red shirt, Amelia. Pink shirt, Beatrice. Yellow

shirt, Cynthia. Green shirt, Darla. Blue shirt, Eleanor. I found a note from Lexi with their names and a bit more information about their lives over the last twenty-eight months. The girls are fraternal—even though they look like carbon copies to me. The kids are actually her stepchildren, but Lexi was given custody soon after her husband's death.'' He paused before adding, ''The note also made it clear that Lexi doesn't plan to retrieve them anytime soon.''

Casey eased toward the toddler—Amelia. Then, sweeping the child into her arms, she checked the toilet water for the minister's personal belongings. Luckily, the shoe seemed to be the only casualty.

Bouncing the baby to divert her from the loss of her latest game, Casey carried her to the sink, washed the little girl's hands, then dried them on a towel that smelled faintly of…

Lavender.

''I don't know how I'll remember all their names,'' she said as she hefted the baby onto her hip again, then shepherded the other two toward the door.

Two. How was she ever going to manage two of her own when they began the ''flushing'' phase of their lives?

''ABCs,'' Stephen explained cryptically.

Rounding the doorway, she peered down at Stephen, wondering how any man could look so completely exhausted and…

So heart-wrenchingly wonderful.

He'd braced his back against the bed and rested

his head against the mattress. Patently exhausted, he hadn't bothered to open his eyes on her return, and his thick lashes swept invitingly over high cheekbones and a jaw covered with dark stubble. One of the toddlers lay in the crook of his arm, head back, mouth open, while another gripped his strong, callused hand as if it were a treasured teddy bear.

For some unaccountable reason—or perhaps because of her own newly aroused instincts for motherhood—Casey had the sudden urge to cry.

Darn it all, she shouldn't be so touched by the sight. She'd never appreciated authority figures of any kind, let alone pastors, priests or gurus. In her experience growing up, she'd found most men of the cloth to be stiff and unyielding, kind but formally distant.

But at that moment, Stephen Dubois looked so approachable, so...human. The vulnerability his weariness inspired clashed with his innate strength. He was completely protective of these five little strangers, and his instinctive tenderness automatically inspired the sharing of secret sorrows and weighty confidences.

So what would he say if I told him how lonely I've been, too?

Casey tried to push the thought aside, but it refused to leave. What *would* Stephen say if she confessed how lonely she'd felt of late? Not just because life seemed to be rushing past her at an alarming rate, but because she'd never really felt in sync with anyone. Certainly not with her own family. Although she loved them dearly and appreciated all they'd taught her, Casey had never enjoyed protest rallies, organically grown produce and living out of a Volkswagen van.

"Don't worry, you'll get the hang of it."

At Stephen's sudden comment, she dragged her mind back to the matter at hand.

"What?" she asked vaguely.

"ABCs. The girls have been named in alphabetical order. Amelia, Beatrice, Cynthia, Darla, Eleanor."

"How very…cute." Casey knew she had no reason to judge how another woman had named her daughters, but there was something almost clinical about an alphabetical list.

"It gets worse," Stephen said, his voice husky from weariness. "According to the letter of instructions I found, Lexi refers to them by their nicknames."

"Which are?"

"Amy, Buffy, Cissy, Didi and Ellie."

As if in response, the sleeping babies twitched. Amy merely grabbed a lock of Casey's hair and tugged.

"Hung-y," the little girl insisted. Her sisters echoed the sentiment.

Since Casey couldn't think of a comment to make about the five nicknames—which sounded like a roll call for debutante wannabes—she said instead, "Would you like me to take this trio with me? I could bathe them and feed them until the others wake. Maybe you could get a few minutes of rest that way."

"That," he said in a dark, rumbling voice that made her stomach knot in anticipation, "would be the most wonderful thing that anyone has ever offered to do for me."

"Oh, really?"

"Mmm." He sounded as if he were half asleep already. "I can't ever remember receiving a better pro...po...si...tion...."

His chest lifted and fell in a deep, weary sigh.

"Judging by that remark, you don't get out much."

Knowing Stephen's chances for sleep would be slim over the next few days, she moved around the pastor's quarters as quietly as she could. Searching through the rubble, she managed to find diapers, wipes, undershirts and a change of clothing.

One change of clothing per child. How odd.

Unless Speedy Delivery would be making another stop at the rectory.

"Come on, Amy, Didi, Cissy," she whispered. "We'll leave Father Stephen to his rest."

She expected one last pithy reply from Stephen's direction—or at least a reminder that he was a pastor, not a father—but the man had fallen asleep.

But as she took one last glance at Stephen, she realized that he had suddenly inherited the right to be called "father."

Father of five. *Five.*

And he was as unprepared for multiple offspring as she.

So keep your hands and your thoughts to yourself, Casey Fairchild. He's completely off-limits—and you should be glad. What woman in her right mind would contemplate a relationship with a man who'd suddenly been saddled with quintuplets?

Especially since the thought of two more babies added to the fold would be enough to drive any man to drink.

Chapter Five

Casey and the three girls shared a delightful morning together. They walked through the gardens, explored the chapel, played ball on the lawn—and even helped Anne deadhead roses.

The girls, who had been drawn time and time again to the "flowers" growing on the front lawn, had picked a ragged bouquet of dandelions and presented them to Anne. To Casey's relief and delight, the older woman solemnly thanked the toddlers for the gift, then displayed the weeds in a jelly jar, which she placed in the middle of the kitchen table.

Since the sparse breakfast Casey had eaten—supplemented only by a share of the toddlers' own meal of cereal and sliced bananas—wore off soon before noon, Casey volunteered to make lunch.

Anne tried to protest—the word *duty* cropping up from time to time, but Casey insisted. After all, she'd already had a sample of the woman's cooking, and visions of a menu of gruel and water kept prodding Casey to remain firm.

In the end, Anne relented—although the wrestling highlights on cable television probably swayed Casey's argument.

As soon as the woman settled into her chair, Casey hurried to the kitchen to investigate the cupboards. Throughout her efforts, she continued a running monologue for the girls' benefit.

The little girls giggled and chattered in return, all the while sitting on stools that Casey had made into makeshift high chairs by pulling them close to the table and tying the children in place with dish towels.

It was obvious that Amy and her sisters were enjoying the attentions of an adult without having to compete with the rest of their sisters. After dining on juice, SpaghettiOs and toast, the toddlers dragged Casey through the rectory, intent on exploring such fascinating things as the cord to the vacuum cleaner, the cut-crystal knobs on the doors and the slippery hardwood floors. Funny, but Casey had never really paid much attention to anything so close to the ground before.

By four in the afternoon, however, Casey was praying for the pastor's return. She'd thought he and the rest of the quintuplets would sleep for an hour at the most, not the whole day. Her own trio of children was showing signs of needing a nap and Casey would soon be left to her own devices.

And the incessant phone calls.

Since Casey still hadn't been told her official duties, she'd begun answering the phone as a matter of habit. By the third call she'd endured, she had sensed an obvious pattern.

Somehow, the small-town grapevine—which worked with great efficiency in Ruckerville—had delivered the mixed-up message that the pastor had a new assistant, and that assistant had five little daughters.

Casey was unclear as to how her own arrival by car could have been muddled with the same-day delivery of the girls. But then she realized that the pastor had never really explained to the president of the Ladies' Aid Society how the children had come so abruptly to his home. Nola, who evidently had the imagination of a novelist, had supposed that the quintuplets belonged to Casey and that the pastor had invited her into his home—a young, single, overburdened mother—due to his pity for her situation.

A few minutes after noon, Casey had begun to receive all sorts of offers to help with the children. At first, she'd been impressed with the generosity of the women of Ruckerville. Then she'd begun to note that the services being offered were made by very young, very personable women—and the offers of the baby-sitting services were only made once the ladies determined the pastor was nearby.

It didn't take a rocket scientist to see that the women were merely hoping to spotlight their mothering capabilities with the bachelor pastor. If it had been up to her, Casey would have sold tickets and let the women have their way with Stephen.

But since she didn't feel that it was her place to

explain the sudden appearance of the children or their relationship to the town's minister, she bit her tongue and took reams of messages.

After all, it wouldn't help matters with her future support groups if she alienated the very people she'd been hired to help.

Finally, at ten minutes after four, Stephen Dubois appeared in the doorway of the kitchen, where Casey was feeding Amy, Cissy and Didi a snack comprised of tiny bites of a peanut-butter-and-honey sandwich.

His expression was so sheepish and apologetic, Casey's stomach dipped as if she'd taken a steep plunge on a runaway roller coaster.

"Sorry about that," Stephen said, with a shrug in the direction of his quarters.

She waved aside his apology. "You needed the rest."

"Yes, but today is your first in Ruckerville, and I should have taken the time to introduce you to some people and show you around."

"I doubt you could have stayed awake for any sort of a formal presentation."

He grimaced. "You're probably right."

"Where are the rest of the children?"

"Still asleep, if you can believe it. They must be fighting jet lag." He grimaced. "It's probably their exhaustion that's kept them so easy to manage so far, so brace yourself."

Casey took a wet dishcloth and wiped the girls' hands and faces.

"These three will be out for the count soon

enough. They've been fighting a nap for the past thirty minutes, but I think they're ready to collapse,'' Casey murmured.

Amy escaped Casey's grasp and reached for the remains of her sandwich, swirling her fingers in the streaks of peanut butter and revising the designs she'd already made with the sticky goo.

Stephen stared at the infants' high chairs—one that was obviously new and expensive. ''Where did that come from?''

''Let's see...'' Casey thought for a moment, reviewing the parade of visitors who had appeared at the rectory door in the past hour. Evidently, when the women's phone campaigns hadn't achieved any tangible results, some of the marriage candidates had felt compelled to offer even more assistance— whether it be in the form of baby paraphernalia or food.

''This high chair came from Mrs. Midgley—who sent it by way of her eldest daughter Fran.''

Casey captured Amy's hands and wiped them clean again. ''The others came by way of the eldest daughters of Mrs. Greer, Mrs. Roberts, Mrs. Thayne and Mrs. Thompson. They have very *lovely* daughters, by the way.''

Stephen grimaced, and if she wasn't mistaken, a slight stain of red began to work its way up his throat.

''Besides the chairs, we've been graced with three playpens, a baby pool, several boxes of clothing, bottles, toys, cakes, cookies, casseroles, pies, jars of homemade baby food and a life-size stuffed cow.''

"Life-size?"

"Nearly."

She threw the washcloth into the sink, then lifted Amy and planted her on her hip while she gestured for Stephen to shepherd Cissy and Didi. ''You've got quite a generous congregation, Father Dubois.''

"Pas—''

''I'd wager you and the rest of the occupants of the rectory won't need to cook for the better part of a month.''

He shifted, an audacious smile spreading over his lips. ''Actually, we rarely cook.''

She tried not to meet his grin with one of her own, but she couldn't keep her expression from cracking.

''I take it the food is a usual occurrence.''

He winked. ''I've been told I'm quite a catch in the community.''

''I bet,'' she offered ruefully. ''So which of the likely bridal candidates have captured your eye?''

He tipped his head back, pretending to think. ''Let's see…Sherry Dunne makes a fantastic cobbler, Donna Cooper has a lasagna that can make a man speak in tongues.''

''Italian being one of them, of course,'' Casey quipped.

''Rhonda Rawlins has this seven-layer salad that is a hit during Monday night football with the boys, Louella Simpson—''

''Spare me the list of gastronomical delights. Isn't

there a single woman to enter the confines of the rectory who's piqued anything more than your appetite?''

Casey supposed it was bold of her to speak to her employer in such an informal manner, but there was something about Stephen Dubois that made her feel as if she'd known him much longer than a day. And try as she might to behave in a calm, respectable, professional manner, she couldn't seem to tame her own natural exuberance.

Stephen regarded her for several unsettling minutes, then offered, ''Not until very recently.''

If Casey were conceited enough, she supposed that she might fall into that category.

Of course, she'd never lacked for ego.

Especially when the look the pastor offered her was so direct, so laden with meaning, so…heady, she couldn't tear her own gaze away.

''Those babies are up,'' a voice announced from the doorway to the summer porch.

Both Stephen and Casey jumped at Anne's sudden announcement. Although they did their best to look casual, Casey was sure they looked guilty as hell.

Anne shot a stern stare at each of them and marched to the refrigerator.

''Frankly, I think that someone should go get them,'' the elderly woman muttered.

Stephen sighed, and the intimate mood was shattered.

''I'm on my way,'' he said, heading for his rooms,

but Anne stopped him before he'd taken more than a couple of steps.

"It's too late for that."

"For what?" Stephen asked, glancing over his shoulder.

"They aren't in your quarters anymore, Pastor."

"What?"

"From what I could tell by the noise, they were climbing onto the roof and heading for the tree house."

Stephen swore and ran from the rectory.

Casey quickly followed, clutching Amy to her as if the baby were in similar danger. All the while, her heart hammered in her chest and a light-headedness threatened to make her too dizzy to move.

But as soon as she had run far enough away from the house and looked up at the roof, she realized why Anne hadn't seemed overly concerned by the toddlers' antics. The windows in question opened onto a large veranda completely surrounded by an intricate railing and leading to an adjoining tree house.

Since Casey had arrived at the rectory after dark, she hadn't really had a chance to fully examine the structure until now. In the brilliant afternoon sunshine, she was able to see that the parish house was actually several buildings of differing styles that had been connected in a haphazard way to form a delightful jumble of architecture.

From here, she was able to clearly distinguish the rough sandstone bricks from the original rectory, as well as the square, high-pitched roof of the addition that formed the east wing and the boarding area.

Behind and to the south was a portion apparently added at the turn of the century, judging by the gingerbread trim, Gothic towers and archways.

"That's the cultural center," Anne said, intercepting the direction of Casey's gaze. "There's a newly remodeled kitchen, full-size gym, meeting rooms and office space, but nearly a hundred years ago, it was the chapel."

Warming to her self-imposed role of tour guide, Anne said, "I suppose you've noted the original structure where your own room is located. If you look closely, you can see the date 1864 carved into one of the bricks just below your sill."

Anne then gestured to the spot where the pastor was scaling a set of narrow wooden steps that led up the side of the gnarled trunk of an ancient tree.

"During the thirties, we had a pastor with a large family, so the new section of the rectory was built on his behalf. The structure is art deco in design, as you'll note by the curved walls and the angular details to the windows. The veranda where you see the children playing leads to the flat roof located directly over the pastor's office. Each afternoon, he would climb up a small staircase hidden behind one of the bookshelves on the first floor. His wife was a wonder with flowers, and she designed a roof garden to rival that of any New York apartment house. Ever since that time, succeeding pastors' wives have used the area as a place for meetings and ladies' teas."

Casey absently absorbed the history lesson. Her heart was only just returning to its normal rhythm as she realized the two little girls were in no danger whatsoever—especially since she caught sight of the two elderly companions who were playing with them.

"Hello there!"

Just as Stephen dodged into the tree house, Bert's head popped into view in one of the window openings.

Stephen paused in his mad dash, obviously relieved, and Casey exhaled the breath she hadn't even known she'd held.

"Send the other little tikes up here, Miss Fairchild," Bert called. "We're having a grand time playing."

"I think they're ready for a nap," Casey advised.

He waved aside the comment as if it were of no importance—and to her amazement, Myrtle giggled and gestured to Amy, Cissy and Didi.

"Come up, come up!"

Bert added his own incentives to the plan. "We've got blankets and a jug of lemonade and some blocks to keep the babies busy. I'm sure we can make a nest for your set of little ones. They'll drop off once they're good and ready."

Casey supposed she should continue to protest, but she was ready for some peace and quiet—and a snack of her own. She had a horrible craving for salty French fries—no doubt inspired by Erica's dire warning that Ruckerville was too small for a fast-food chain of any kind.

Carefully, she made her way over the neatly trimmed lawn with its incredible borders of flowers. Herding Cissy and Didi ahead of her, she scaled the narrow steps that led to the tree house. Soon, it became apparent that the structure hadn't been constructed haphazardly, but had been carefully designed and bolted into place.

As she neared Stephen, he relieved her of the babies' care and passed the sleepy toddlers to Bert.

"There you are, my precious babies," Bert cooed.

Myrtle frowned at him and shouted, "What?"

Behind her, Buffy and Ellie parroted, "What, what, what, what, what…" giving the impression of baby ducklings quacking at their leader.

Casey was debating whether she should volunteer to stay with the elderly couple, but Stephen grasped her hand and began pulling her toward the roof garden.

"If you don't mind serving as baby-sitters, I'll take a few minutes to introduce Casey to her duties as my assistant."

Bert waved the comment aside. "Take your time—take her to lunch! It's so nice to have wee ones at the rectory again."

"Thanks, Bert."

Stephen ushered Casey to ground level. Then—as if fearing that Bert and Myrtle would change their minds, he pulled her in the direction of a battered Suburban.

"Hurry before the pitter-patter of little feet starts following us."

But as Casey hurried after the pastor, she wondered if any of them realized that there would be no dearth of the "pitter-patter of little feet" at the rectory for some time.

In fact, Casey would soon be adding another two pair to the din.

Chapter Six

Stephen took Casey to the town's only café, a tiny one-story building that, he informed her, had been connected to the bowling alley until a freak winter storm had collapsed the rest of the building, leaving the eating establishment completely untouched.

Despite the late-afternoon hour, the restaurant was filled with people, and at least a dozen more waited outside the door for an available table. But the moment Stephen was seen in line, the hostess—sporting an enormous beehive hairstyle, bright orange lipstick and a name tag reading Flossy—came to retrieve him.

''Pastor Dubois, you know you don't have to stand out here in the wind. Come on inside. I've got a nice corner booth all fixed up for you and your assistant. Welcome to Ruckerville, Miss Fairchild.''

Casey didn't bother to ask how the woman had learned her identity and occupation. She supposed that, like in a city of any size, the most common forms of debriefing occurred in restaurants, beauty shops and hardware stores.

Stephen tried to object, but the men in coveralls and women in housedresses and jeans, urged him to eat while he had the time.

They were shown to a booth made of brilliant red Naugahyde trimmed in chrome and repaired with strips of duct tape. As they settled into their places, Flossy handed them both menus that were neatly typed and encased in plastic sleeves.

Casey wasn't sure what she'd expected to find as she studied her choices, but she was soon delighted by the plethora of food being offered—all at a third of what a similar meal would have cost in Manhattan.

"I've died and gone to my grandmother's kitchen," she murmured, her stomach growling as she read the descriptions of soups, sandwiches, salads, hot meals and desserts. There was no lack of "meat and potatoes" for hungry farmers or "slim concoctions" for the ladies.

"Have whatever strikes your fancy—everything's good. But make sure you save room for pie, or Flossy will take offense and think she hasn't fed you properly.

Casey's mouth watered.

What to eat…what to eat…

Meat loaf sandwiches, hot turkey plates with mashed potatoes and gravy, cottage fries, shepherd's pie, grilled pork chops, stuffed tomatoes, chili, five kinds of soup…

The possibilities were endless, each one bringing

to mind the cooking deified by mealtimes with *Leave It to Beaver*'s mom, Mayberry's Aunt Bea or *Bonanza*'s Hop Sing.

"God bless America," she said under her breath, then started when a grizzled farmer in a neighboring booth responded with "Amen."

Grinning, she waggled her fingers at the man, and he blushed and offered a wave of his own.

"Tell me, Miss Fairchild. Do you have this effect on all men?"

She blinked at Stephen in surprise.

"What effect?"

"You tend to completely disarm us."

Us? Did that mean that the pastor found her somehow…intriguing?

Or merely annoying?

"I'm sure I don't know what you mean," she insisted archly.

"Oh, but I think you do."

Thankfully, Flossy's arrival interrupted any further comments Stephen might have made.

Scrambling to make up her mind, Casey ordered the blue plate special—a hot turkey sandwich with roasted Dutch oven potatoes, cracked wheat rolls, peach preserves, soup, salad and a side of gravy.

In a moment, Flossy suddenly appeared, carrying a pair of heavy crockery bowls filled to the brim with chicken noodle soup. The broth was laden with every vegetable imaginable, thick chunks of chicken and hand-rolled noodles. After only one bite, Casey gave up fast-food chains forever and swore her allegiance to Flossy's Café.

As Casey dug into her dinner, sighing in delight at each bite of the incredible soup, Stephen reached into the satchel he'd brought with him. Using the large table as a desk, he spread out several colorful folders, then handed Casey a three-ring binder printed with the church's name and logo.

"This is for you. Inside, you'll find copies of the yearly calendar, notes from the last few planning meetings, mission statements for our social and educational groups, and an outline of your duties. I've also included a sample prospectus we've developed for a government grant. Our community is in desperate need of a day care and educational center for the migrant children who move in and out of the area. If you don't mind my stretching the boundaries of your job to one of my secular committees, I'd like your input on what we've developed so far, as well as any ideas you might have that could strengthen the request."

He pointed to the shiny folder, explaining, "Feel free to refuse, if you want. The grant isn't part of your official job, since it's a volunteer community-action project. But your expertise would prove valuable if you have the time."

"I'd love to look at it."

"This second folder holds rough outlines of the support groups I'd like you to form. The church already has a fairly strong youth group that meets bi-weekly. But as it stands, the activities we plan for the teenagers are more for socializing than anything else. The special-interest groups you'll be organizing will remain separate from what we're already doing."

Casey thumbed through the pages, impressed by the professional presentation of her responsibilities, the church's policy and procedures, the lists of goals and the background information provided about those individuals who would be invited to join her programs. Before joining WMMN, Casey had worked with several private clinics and detox centers, and she couldn't remember any of them having this much employment detail finished and documented before her arrival.

Stephen finished his own soup and set the bowl aside. "I want you to know how much I appreciate your willingness to come to Ruckerville and take the job. After advertising for nearly a year, I didn't think we'd ever get an interested nibble, let alone someone who would actually move here."

"Your cousin was very…persuasive."

"Madge Beaman can get that way."

So it was Erica's mother who had done all the talking.

"I hope Madge didn't tie you to a chair to pitch the position."

Casey laughed at the image. Erica's mother was a very determined woman, and Stephen was obviously well aware of the fact.

"No. She didn't. Actually, it was her daughter who informed me of the opening."

"Ahh, yes. Anna…Esther…"

"Erica," Casey supplied. "I take it you haven't met."

Stephen shook his head. "The Beaman cousins are from my mother's side of the family. There must be a hundred of them."

"Hardly."

"Sometimes it seems that way," he said, his eyes twinkling. "Now that I think of it, Madge said you'd been told about the job because you were recuperating or something. Erica must be a doctor like the rest of them."

Casey's heart lurched in her chest. Here was her chance. She'd just been given the perfect opportunity to confess that Erica was an obstetrician and Casey was her patient.

"What were you told about my…health?" she asked slowly. Carefully. Wondering if her rapport with this man was about to shatter into a million pieces. The announcement of twins seemed to have that effect on people. Especially men.

"All I know is, whatever you have, it isn't catching," he said, clearly curious.

Not in the literal sense of the word, no.

"I…had some minor surgery, you might say," Casey said, feeling as if she were treading over a verbal minefield.

"Is there anything I need to know?"

Yes. I'm pregnant. I'm very pregnant. And I still find you sexy as hell and would like nothing more than to pull you across the table and kiss you.

Casey gasped at her own thoughts. Where had that impulse come from? She really would have to talk to Erica about her hormone levels. This outlandish behavior—outlandish even for her—couldn't possibly be normal.

She cleared her throat and said, "You see, Erica...well, she treats women who..."

Stephen cleared his throat and held up a hand. "Say no more. I think I get the picture. You were treated for what my mother delicately called 'female problems.'"

"Well, in a way—"

"It's none of my business, and I have no desire to make you feel uncomfortable. All I want is your promise that you won't let me tax your strength in any way."

"There's no likelihood of that. I tend to tire easily lately, but I'm healthy as a horse. As a matter of fact—"

"Good. Then we'll drop the subject and move on to another. I think that Madge was quite up front with you in regards to the salary we're offering and the part-time status of your job. Right now, we can't afford to pay you to work full-time—although in time, if the demand for your services increases, we'll see about extending your hours. In the meantime, I don't expect or want you to work beyond the fifteen hours a week we've proposed."

Casey stared at Stephen, her mouth parted.

The moment had passed. Gone was her perfect chance to confess her pregnancy.

And she wasn't sure if she was disappointed or relieved.

With some effort, she dragged her attention back to her job and the responsibilities Stephen was outlining.

"I think that in the short time you've been here," Stephen was saying, "you've also seen that organizing some sort of routine at the rectory is all but impossible for me. As my assistant, you won't be required to keep set hours. Instead, I'll leave a list of things I need done in my office and you can schedule your own time."

"Fine."

"I would like the support groups to meet regularly, however."

"I'd planned on set days and times for each of the sessions."

"Good. I think such a plan will offer a sense of stability to those involved. Once you've had a chance to go through the files and come up with your own strategies, I'll arrange whatever you need in regards to a meeting space."

He leaned forward as if imparting a secret. "Just keep in mind that Ruckerville is like any other close-knit community. *Nothing* interferes with high school varsity sporting events. The girls' and boys' varsity baseball teams are three games away from the state tournament, and Ruckerville becomes a ghost town twenty minutes before the opening pitch. I'd also steer clear of the firemen's trout fest, city league soccer, and any choir or band performances."

"I'll try to remember that," Casey said, wondering if she had found some down-home version of Shangri-la. What more could a person ask for?

Flossy arrived with their meals, and as Casey forked steaming turkey and gravy into her mouth, she wondered if she'd somehow hallucinated this whole experience. Had she actually heard her employer insist she take afternoons and weekends off? If so, she'd stumbled across a tiny corner of heaven.

Suddenly, the smell of bus exhaust, traffic, bleating telephones and the overwhelming desire to push herself to the top of the entertainment ladder seemed very far away. For the first time in her life, Casey was being forced to see how her life had revolved around her career for too long. Now that she'd been ordered to relax and slow down, she was discovering that she was more than happy with the arrangement. Upon learning she carried twins, her priorities had shifted, and it suddenly became more important to her that she balance her life-style. Besides her work, she needed time to herself and her children, a feeling of belonging, a sense of contentment.

"Well? Can you stand working with us for a little while?" Stephen asked as he summed up his presentation.

A little while? Did it have to end? Or was the job open for the next few hundred years?

"I think I could manage to stick around," she finally managed to say.

There was a beat of silence. Stephen pushed at the crumbs on his plate, but his eyes were on her.

"Do you mind if I ask how long you're thinking of staying in Ruckerville?"

Could the man read her mind?

But as she absorbed the way he looked at her, the glint of interest in his eyes, she realized the question was purely personal.

"I...uh, I don't know," Casey said as she cast covert glances at the patrons, who had made no secret of their curiosity about the pastor's assistant.

"A year? Two?"

"At least a year." She suddenly thought of her babies. She envisioned them living in her cramped Manhattan apartment, taking city transportation to school, walking blocks to the nearest park. But that image was soon superimposed by the green fields of Ruckerville, big yellow school buses, tree-lined streets...

And side orders of gravy.

"It could be longer." She hesitated for an instant, then offered, "Who knows? I may decide to put down roots here."

His smile was slow and so dazzling that she caught her breath.

"That would be nice."

Flossy chose that moment to bring Stephen the check and two take-out boxes of pie. When Casey had insisted she was too full to eat another bite, Flossy had insisted the pastor's assistant "take something home for later."

"Pastor, I wish you'd let me pick up the tab,"

Flossy said as she set the scrap of paper on the table, then refused to let go of it.

"Flossy, we've been through this before. Your food is well worth every penny and more."

"But the way you helped my sister through her divorce." Flossy turned to Casey to say, "He was a rock of strength. Annabelle didn't know what she was going to do when Floyd up and left her, emptied their bank account and took their only car. The pastor here helped her get a job at the factory and fixed up one of the junkers Floyd had resting in the field so that she'd have some independence. Most folk wouldn't go to such extremes. They'd bring her a casserole, pat her hand and say 'There, there.' But eventually, their own lives would take all their time again."

She took a voluminous linen handkerchief from her pocket and wiped her eyes. "Not this man," she said with a flick of her hand in Stephen's direction. "He calls or visits Annabelle at least once or twice a week. I keep telling my sister that she should stop mooning over ol' Floyd and set her sights on the pastor, but she's a shy little thing."

She shook her finger at Stephen. "If you ever decide to settle down, you couldn't do much better than Annabelle, Pastor Dubois. She's not like these flighty women who dally after church and flirt with you on the front steps. She's a solid woman with a will of iron. And her buttermilk brownies…"

"She's too good for me, Flossy," Stephen said, disarming the situation with a wink of his eye. "Besides, you know there isn't a female in town who can cook half as well as you." He placed a hand over his heart. "Alas, you're married. So I'm forced to pine away and dream of your apple dumplings and pot roast."

Flossy blushed like a schoolgirl. "Get on with you now," she said, then giggled like a teenager. Poking Casey with a finger, she offered, "You and your babies will be in good hands with this man. Don't you worry."

Stephen waited until Flossy had moved from earshot before repeating, "You and *your* babies?"

For one horrible instant, Casey thought that her secret had been discovered and that the Ruckerville grapevine had somehow managed to obtain a copy of her ultrasound. But then, as a cool wave of reason washed over her, she remembered the women who had called and visited the rectory. Every one of them had assumed the quintuplets were hers.

So here's another perfect chance to tell him the truth.

No. Not yet. Not until…

Until you're big as a house? Don't you think he'll guess long before then?

Frantically, Casey struggled with her conscience. But before she could settle on a plan of attack, Stephen suddenly frowned.

"They think the quints are yours, don't they?"

"Well, yes. I suppose—"

Sighing, he shook his head. "How in the world

can such simple facts get so hopelessly muddled?'' His hand slid across the table and gripped Casey's.

She bit her lip when the contact caused a rash of gooseflesh to race up her arm.

''Don't worry. I'll get everything straightened out by nightfall. A quick call to Nola Wilkens should get the grapevine working in our favor.''

Worry? Why would she worry? Why would she care what these people thought of her? As far as she was concerned, the entire population of Ruckerville could think she and the quintuplets were aliens from another planet as long as Stephen Dubois continued to touch her hand…absently rub her knuckles…

Then, abruptly, Stephen was moving away. Placing a ten dollar bill on the table, he slid from his seat. ''Come on. I need to give you a tour of the chapel, cultural hall and meeting facilities. Then I suppose I'd better relieve Bert and Myrtle of their baby-sitting responsibilities before the charm of tending the quintuplets wears off.''

JUDGING BY THE WAY BERT, Myrtle and Anne were waiting for them at the front curb, the novelty of having five toddlers to watch had worn off long before Casey and Stephen had finished eating.

Sighing, Stephen supposed the time alone with his new assistant was about to come to an abrupt end. As soon as possible, he would have to start finding a baby-sitter for the girls.

''We've got our study group tonight,'' Anne said,

already heading toward an age-old Chrysler that had been built along the same lines as the *QE2*.

"I thought your meeting wasn't until seven," Stephen said as he swung from his own battered Suburban.

"It isn't," Anne offered succinctly. Then she and her siblings scrunched into the front seat and slammed the doors.

"We're going early so Myrtle can get some peace and quiet," Anne shouted through the window. "The children are in the kitchen with Betty Shupe. She brought you a pie and volunteered to watch the babies until you came home."

Myrtle needed peace and quiet? Stephen thought with a growing sense of dread.

The Chrysler's tires squealed against the pavement as Anne backed out of the driveway, sideswiping a trio of empty garbage cans in the process. Then she sped away at an alarming speed—considering the fact that Stephen had never seen Anne top thirty miles per hour.

As the car screeched around the corner, a niggling sense of unease crept up his spine.

When he glanced at Casey, she shrugged. "I suppose the newness didn't last as long as either of us thought it would."

Stephen approached the rectory steps with something akin to dread. For the past hour, he'd enjoyed being with Casey. She was funny, witty. Best of all, his position as a minister didn't seem to affect her in the least. In fact, his title seemed to make her bolder in her comments, as if she was testing his "shock-ability" factor.

He couldn't remember the last time a woman had intrigued him so completely.

Attracted him.

Invited him.

Casey's lips slid into a crooked smile. "You're staring, Pastor."

"Am I?"

"Yes."

"And how does that make you feel?"

Obviously, she hadn't expected her boldness to be countered with some of his own.

"I don't know..." she admitted slowly. "But I think to continue such a course of action could be dangerous."

"Why is that?"

She spread her arms wide. "The situation we find ourselves in is innately dangerous—a small-town minister, big-city gal."

"I was born and raised in Minneapolis."

"Ahh, but you live here now."

"And you don't think that the community could come to accept you?"

"I think they'll accept me...eventually. But I don't think they'd care for the local pastor to look outside the city limits for his...social needs."

"What if I told you that my congregation had very little say in such matters?"

He was moving toward her, enjoying the way she backed up, step by step. Soon, the stoop would stop her progress and she would have to let him close the distance.

"Don't you think that such…fraternization could be considered unprofessional?"

Did she know how she made his blood begin to ease through his body like hot honey? She was so earnest, every expression, every thought racing transparently across her features. She was excited by his advance, yes, yet still nervous and hesitant and wary.

When had any woman looked at him that way? He'd grown so accustomed to most females regarding him as some sort of father figure or husband material, he'd forgotten how intoxicating it could be to arouse such stark sensual emotions in another person.

"As long as I don't become one of your patients, I don't see how anything…personal between us could be considered inappropriate," he responded.

"But I live in your house…"

"Behind a locked door in a detached wing."

"I will eat meals with you, work with you—"

"All the better to get to know you, my dear," he offered with his best wolfish tone.

She stopped short against the bottom step, just as he'd known she would. Vainly, she held out a hand to prevent him from coming any closer, but the move backfired when her palm came into contact with his chest. Such a muscled chest. Such a masculine chest.

"I—I still think that to regard each other as anything but employer and employee would be a mistake. Eventually, there would be a parting of the ways—"

"Why would you say that?" he murmured, pressing against her until her elbow bent and he was able to close the distance between them.

"Father—"

"Stephen," he corrected her, his head bending. She smelled so good.

"St-Stephen," she stammered. "I don't know if I can—"

He stopped whatever she had been about to say by placing his fingertip against her lips. "Sometimes, the best things in life require a leap of faith," he whispered.

Then he replaced his finger with his lips.

Chapter Seven

In her lifetime, Casey had been kissed by a Little League pitcher, a football captain, a law student, a politician, an actor and an entrepreneur. But nothing had prepared her for the incredible sensations inspired by Stephen Dubois.

Stephen's embrace was achingly sweet, his lips soft against her own, yet forceful enough to fill her veins with a raging heat.

Never in her life had a mere kiss made her knees tremble so hard, she feared they would buckle. As his hands slid around her waist and pulled her against him, molding their bodies chest to chest, she was swamped by a fiery passion. In an instant, she felt adored, invigorated and humbled. He worshipped her mouth, caressed, teased, then bid her to open her lips for a more thorough exploration.

Seeking an anchor in the maelstrom of sensation, she grabbed fistfuls of his sweatshirt. Rising on tiptoe, she deepened the embrace with the tip of her head, the stroke of her tongue against his own lips.

Was it really possible that this man—this near stranger—could fill her with such instant joy? She'd known him such a short time, yet, if he'd asked, she would have allowed him to sweep her into his arms and into his bedroom. And the fact that such an event wasn't likely to happen, due to Stephen's moral code, only heightened the power of his embrace.

Groaning, she gasped for air, releasing him only long enough to plunge her fingers through his hair. So soft, so silken, yet so incredibly masculine.

Stephen's hands slid to her shoulder blades, then down to the small of her back, drawing her hips so tightly to his that she couldn't mistake the depth of his arousal. And when her stomach met with the washboard resistance of his belly, she gulped air into her lungs.

Then froze.

Her stomach. He mustn't hold her so tightly. If he did, if he really understood the reason why her body was not as trim as her clothing might lead him to believe...

He'll know you're pregnant.

A sudden scream shattered the quiet, causing them to jump apart like guilty teenagers.

Stephen was the first to react, wrenching free from a kiss that had been much too brief. Taking the steps two at a time, he whipped the screen door open and disappeared inside.

Unable to move, Casey took deep drags of the cool air.

He hasn't guessed. Your secret is still safe.

But for how long? She had to tell Stephen the truth before she unwittingly hurt him with her reticence.

Casey knew her conscience was right. She had no business allowing Stephen to think that she was free to revel in his attentions.

Still…if things had been different…

So what would you wish away? Your children?

Her fingers curled into a tight fist over the roundness hidden by her jumper. Never. She would never regret the miracle of life that grew inside her. Her twins were so small still, but she loved them with all her heart and soul.

And nothing must get in the way of their health and future happiness.

Not even Stephen Dubois.

Forcing herself to move, Casey wrenched free of the sensual cocoon that still clouded her brain. But it was the sound of shattering glass that sent her running toward whatever catastrophe awaited them all.

Bursting through the screen doorway, she skidded to a halt in the entrance of the parlor. As her eyes roamed the room, she found a woman about her own age huddled on the couch. Betty Shupe, Casey supposed. The stranger was openly weeping and clutched a dishcloth to her face to absorb the tears that cascaded down her cheeks. Around her were shards of bric-a-brac from the étagère that had been upended on the floor.

The quintuplets—led by the ever-eager Amy— were squealing and racing around the parlor, beating spoons against pans and aluminum bowls that they had presumably found in the kitchen.

Stephen grabbed Ellie by the straps of her overalls, then Didi, but the other three children managed to elude him. Soon, Stephen's shouts, the frustrated yells of the captured toddlers, the banging of the pans and poor Betty's weeping reached an ear-crashing level.

Knowing that something had to be done, Casey made a beeline for Amy. Hefting the toddler into her arms, Casey tapped the baby on the tip of her nose and sternly said, "No."

Amy's squeals instantly died. Wide-eyed, she stared at Casey—clearly flabbergasted her friend would speak to her so firmly.

"Nice girls don't behave like this," Casey continued, wondering all the while if Amy would decide to attempt an escape—or retaliate by biting her outstretched finger.

But Amy grew still and forlorn.

"No?" she whispered.

"No," Casey said again—employing the same tone Sister Mary Simon used in the parochial school when Casey had been caught sliding down the polished banister in the front lobby.

Holding her breath, Casey prayed that the scolding would subdue the child long enough for the other children to follow suit. The noise level was definitely tapering off.

But to Casey's horror, Amy's eyes filled with tears and her chin wobbled.

"Bad? I bad?"

Sensing the change, the other girls quieted and turned to see what was happening to their ringleader. When Amy began to cry, huge tears rolling down her cheeks, her sisters sank to the floor, eyes wide.

Casey was feeling about as low as a worm, but she didn't dare back down.

"Amy, I think you should say you're sorry to Ms. Shupe."

Amy looked at Casey, her tears abating as she scowled. It was clear by the little girl's expression that she thought Casey's request was untenable. But when Casey refused to relent, Amy finally rested her head on Casey's shoulder, peered at the other woman under her lashes and whispered, "'O-ry."

Close enough.

"Buffy, why don't you say you're sorry as well."

Buffy hung her head and picked at a piece of fluff on the carpet.

"Ms. Shupe is waiting."

"'O-ry."

"Cissy?"

Cissy burst into tears, so Stephen jumped in, nudging the girl who clung to his knees.

"You need to say you're sorry, too."

The grumbling whispers weren't entirely gracious, but since Casey was amazed that the first attempt at discipline hadn't backfired, she said, "Now, I want all of you in the bathroom so that I can wash your hands and faces. March."

Taking her literally, the quintuplets jumped to their

feet. As Amy scrambled loose, they stamped their way in the general direction of the bathroom under the stairs.

Casey winked at Stephen, then said, "I'll just leave the two of you to..." Since Betty Shupe was still sobbing, she finished lamely, "Whatever. Feel free to take whatever time you need."

JUDGING BY THE SPEED with which Betty Shupe left the rectory that night, even the pastor's charming personality hadn't been able to smooth her ruffled feathers—and after a few weeks with the quintuplets in residence, Casey was beginning to see why.

To say that the quintuplets had more than the average amount of energy was an understatement. To say that they were obedient and well behaved was an out-and-out lie.

It soon became clear to all of the occupants of the rectory that the quintuplets were not accustomed to being held in check in any way. They openly defied authority, had developed tantrums to an art form and were happiest when they were making a mess.

In the few weeks they'd been in residence at the rectory, they'd gone through two baby-sitters, spilled water from Casey's goldfish bowl, broken three windows, plugged up two toilets and completely dismantled the television set—just in time for Thursday night's *Wrestle Mania.*

After missing her beloved wrestling matches, Anne had grown more dour and taciturn than usual.

Moreover, she refused to inhabit the same room as the children.

Bert, on the other hand, had entered his second childhood. But an hour or two of the quintuplets generally resulted in the need for a long nap.

Myrtle…

Well, Myrtle turned off her amplifier and refused to acknowledge that the children even existed.

Grinning, Casey made her way through the tangled corridors to the cultural hall, where she was scheduled to meet for the first time with her divorced mothers support group.

So far, of all the residents in the rectory, the pastor was faring the best—but it was apparent that even his nerves were wearing thin. With the help of the Ladies' Aid—and a half-dozen single women—he'd installed five youth bunks in his quarters. But the quintuplets were obviously used to being imprisoned in cribs, because they refused to stay put, and judging by the noise coming from the west wing, the pastor spent most of his nights trying to corral them.

Then there was mealtime. Five high chairs, five grouchy, irritable, hungry children. Five sets of busy spoons and messy hands. Invariably, a food fight ensued, and Stephen emerged from the kitchen looking like he'd been wresting alligators in a bowl of mixed Jello-O.

Even so, Casey couldn't fault him for his tenacity. He seemed to honestly want what was best for the babies, even if it meant sacrificing his own peace of mind.

Humming to herself, Casey whipped open the door to meeting room A, then froze when she found nine women—ranging in age from early twenties to mid-fifties—already waiting for her.

"Hello," she said hurriedly. The door she'd so recently thrown open snapped back on its hinges and smacked her in the behind. Grimacing, she glanced at the clock on the wall.

"You're all early."

"We wanted to get a look at you," one woman stated, folding her arms and scowling through lashes that had been lined with a startling shade of electric blue.

"How...sweet," Casey said lamely.

"Yeah, we wanted to see the pastor's woman," another figure chimed.

Casey's gaze bounced from one suspicious female to the next. "There must be some mistake. I am *not* the pastor's woman."

"Nola Wilkens says you are."

Casey couldn't help snorting at that remark, and when she caught one of the women hiding a quick smile, she decided not to apologize for the reaction.

"Do you mean to tell me you're the only single woman in Ruckerville who hasn't set her sights on the pastor?" a tall, stately blonde asked as she swirled her fingertips over her protruding stomach, causing the motto on her T-shirt—I Was Due Three Months Ago, So Don't Ask—to swirl and dance.

Casey was so alarmed, she couldn't help herself. "Are you...really three months overdue?"

The blonde grinned. "Only in spirit, honey."

An older woman with a ghastly polyester print blouse demanded, "Well? Are you after the pastor or not?"

Casey set the oversize sack she'd been carrying on the front table and approached the group.

"Frankly, if circumstances were different, I'd probably chase that man barefoot over hot coals. But at this point in my life, adding a man to my problems would be tantamount to a self-inflicted lobotomy. Besides which, he has recently inherited five children—*five*—and that thought scares me spitless."

There was a moment of stunned silence. Obviously the women hadn't expected Casey to be so candid.

Finally, a regal-looking African American woman smiled wide and gestured to one of the chairs. "Have a seat, Doc. My name's Maggie. What's in the bag?"

Casey grinned, sensing she'd just found several friends among the divorced mothers support group. "Since this is our first get-together, I brought us all a little something to help break the ice."

STEPHEN STRODE THROUGH the shadowy corridors of the cultural hall, hoping to high heaven that the quintuplets hadn't made their way this far when they'd managed to escape. All he needed was for the five little girls to interrupt Casey's first gathering with the divorced mothers.

A thumping noise alerted him, and he headed toward the second floor, but as he topped the landing, he realized it wasn't the twins making the noise, but the low throb of drums and bass guitar.

"What in the world?" he muttered to himself as he made his way to the only door where light trickled through the frosted glass.

Turning the knob as quietly as he could, he peered around the edge, stopped, then stared.

"What is going on here?"

At his voice, the women lounging on the floor turned to face him, and he was immediately inundated with invitations to come in.

Knowing that he wouldn't have been able to turn away even if his hair was on fire, Stephen stepped inside, his eyes growing wide as he absorbed the sight of the women sitting cross-legged on the floor, an upended paper bag of toys between them. From the midst of a fragrant haze, they dressed Barbie dolls, colored with crayons and erected Lego sculptures. On the front table lay the remains of a delivery pizza, cans of soda and a half-dozen candy bar wrappers.

Peering into the cloud of smoke, Stephen located the boom box and a collection of brass bowls wafting something that smelled like...

Like what?

Stephen wasn't sure, but he did know that the scent was weaving its way through his brain and causing a very curious, very...sensual reaction.

Locating his assistant, Stephen pointed to the hall. "Could I see you outside for a moment?"

"Sure."

Casey rolled to her feet, revealing that she'd removed her shoes.

The moment they were cocooned by the relative privacy of the corridor, Stephen whispered, "What the hell do you think you're doing in there?"

"I'm beginning to believe you only use profanity when I'm around. Is it because I'm not a member of your congregation? Or do I really irritate you that much?"

Stephen took a deep breath, holding it in his lungs.

"You don't irritate me," he finally admitted, forcibly calming himself.

"Then what do I do?"

Hadn't anyone told her that pastors weren't accustomed to being spoken to so…so…frankly?

No. Enticingly.

"You continually pull the rug from under my usual composure."

Rather than appearing contrite, she allowed herself a smug grin. "How wonderful."

Planting his hands on his hips, Stephen did his best to remember what had caused him to call her into the hall in the first place.

"Is there something illegal going on in there?"

Her brows rose. "Not that I know of."

"That smoke—"

"Aromatherapy."

"Smells like—"

"Patouli."

Patouli? What on earth was that?

His confusion must have been evident, because she

patted his shoulders as if he were a little boy who'd just been told the circus had left town.

"Relax, Father—"

"Pastor."

"Whatever." She giggled. "I can't believe you'd think that I would offer a group of divorced women some sort of mind-altering substance. That *was* what you were thinking, wasn't it?"

When she phrased his concerns that way, he felt like an idiot. "Well, I...uh..."

"Welcome to the twentieth century, where holistic medicine is finally being combined with science."

She looped her arm through his elbow and began leading him toward the staircase—just as if they were about to take an evening stroll.

"Data shows that recently divorced women are immensely vulnerable to outside stimuli. This hypersensitivity to the darker emotions merely intensifies the inherent confusion caused by their feelings of animosity, isolation and fear. Therefore, it is important that in our support group we foster a climate of unconditional acceptance."

"That doesn't explain the pa...the smoke."

"Patouli is well known for the way it soothes and energizes."

"The dolls?"

"Play therapy. Women are born to nurture, but a divorce often stifles that instinct."

"The braids?"

"Connecting with the inner child."

"The pizza?"

"We were hungry. And if your next question is about the chocolate, it's because we're women. All women like chocolate. We *need* chocolate. The urge cannot be denied, especially in times of stress."

She released him as Stephen took the first step. In truth, he felt like a fool.

"I guess it's been a while since I brushed up on my psychology."

Standing on the step above him, her feet bare, Casey was at eye level, and he immediately caught the hint of mischief in her eyes. "Trust me. None of this would work if you'd tried it with those women."

"Why?"

"You're a man."

"What does that have to do with anything?"

"You're the enemy."

The response tripped so blithely from her tongue that his eyes narrowed.

"What exactly does that mean?"

She shrugged. "Those women have all been on their own for less than a year. They aren't feeling too kindly toward anyone with a Y chromosome at this point."

"I see." Grasping the handrail, he rested one foot on the landing, effectively boxing Casey into an intimate space.

"And is that what *you* think as well? That I'm the enemy?"

"I'm not divorced."

"No. But there's still something…wary about you

whenever I'm nearby. These past few days, I haven't even seen you."

"Maybe it's your aftershave."

"I don't wear aftershave."

"Oh."

He grinned. "What's the matter, Casey? Can't you think of a witty way to disarm the situation?"

"Give me a minute, I'm still thinking."

He touched her lips with his finger. "Don't bother. I'll just take your silence to mean that you don't find me completely untenable."

Then, while the light of sensual awareness flooded into her expression, he beat a hasty retreat.

CASEY WAITED UNTIL the pastor's footsteps had disappeared in the direction of his office before daring to breathe deeply.

"Can you say *quintuplets,* boys and girls?" a voice teased in a Mister Rogers-like tone.

Turning, Casey flushed when she saw all nine women peering curiously at her from the doorway to the meeting room. Maggie, who had uttered the comment, shook her finger and made a tsking noise.

"Maybe *you* think that chasing Pastor Dubois would be the equivalent of a self-inflicted lobotomy," Maggie murmured, the all-knowing grin she wore reflected in her tone. "But I think the pastor's got his own ideas."

AFTER BEING CAUGHT by her support group, Casey did her best to avoid Stephen for the next few days.

But with her job as his assistant and living within the same house, the task was well-nigh impossible.

It was obvious that Stephen thought the children were responsible for her attempts at becoming invisible. Bit by bit they'd wreaked havoc over the rectory, so that even the parade of single women with pies, cakes and homemade casseroles had ebbed to a trickle.

If he knew the truth about her feelings for the girls, Casey was sure she'd be in real hot water. The quintuplets were tricky to handle at first, but Casey was already beginning to distinguish them by personality rather than the color of their shirts. Amy was the ringleader—especially when trouble was involved. Buffy was the adventurer, Cissy the peacemaker. Didi was sensitive and shy. And Ellie merely wanted to be loved.

Although Stephen had hired a full-time baby-sitter for the quints, Casey spent many of her free time hours with them. The girls were a little better behaved, but not much. At the very least, they had begun to realize that when she said no, a consequence for disobedience was attached.

But, rather than causing friction, the rules caused the girls to react in a way that was telling and heartbreaking. It was clear that they hadn't had a stable authority figure in their life for some time. Casey supposed they'd been shuffled from place to place until Lexi had sent them to the rectory.

Even so, Casey was careful to balance her sternness with an abundance of hugs, tickles and story-telling. And in the process, the little girls convinced her that she might—*might*—be able to handle twins of her own.

Casey stepped from the chapel, an empty basket swinging from her arm, the scent of cut flowers still clinging to her hands.

Knowing that the congregation was still wondering what her real role was as "assistant," Casey had used the cuttings from the garden to decorate the choir seats, pulpit and front entrance for the midweek evening services.

So far, despite the fact that she'd been in the pastor's employ for nearly a month, she still hadn't heard one of his sermons—and she knew that the parishioners were beginning to suspect she was an out-and-out heathen.

Actually, due to her eclectic education in regards to God and religion, Casey would have loved to hear Stephen preach. But so far, she'd resisted, knowing that if she saw Stephen in his clerical robes and heard him expound on the mysteries of the Almighty, she would be unable to see him as anything *but* a minister.

Then she would have to admit that dating such a man, kissing him, lusting after him, was somehow sacrilegious.

"Casey!"

A little face appeared in the window of the rectory and she waved to Buffy, but the little girl frantically motioned for her to come.

"Sick. Sick!"

Panic shot through Casey's body and she burst into a run. What had happened now?

Casey had tried to "childproof" the rectory over the past few days, but the quintuplets were experts at moving chairs—and even tables—when they felt they needed something out of their reach.

As soon as she entered the kitchen, she heard the screams and shouts from upstairs. Without thinking, she dropped the basket on the table and rushed in the direction of Stephen's quarters.

But when she skidded to a halt in the doorway of his quarters, it was to discover that the girls weren't in pain, but were hopping up and down in excitement as they surrounded Stephen.

"What's wrong?" she asked.

He looked up, his eyes alight with wonder. "We have babies."

"More babies?" Casey exclaimed in horror. "Now what did Speedy Delivery bring?"

Stephen laughed. "Not *those* sorts of babies. These sorts."

He held up a bundle of rags to expose a tiny pink body not much bigger than his thumb.

"We have mice?" she asked in distaste.

"No," he answered indulgently. "We have rabbits."

Immediately, Casey understood the reason for the fuss. Moving into the room, she joined the children, who huddled around Rabbit's cage as Stephen set the squirming baby animal next to its mother and latched the cage door behind him.

Casey quickly counted the litter.

"Eight," Stephen supplied before she could finish.

"One for each girl, and three to give away," Bert offered as he materialized from the direction of the bathroom. He was screwing the lid on the water bottle. "Maybe you should find yourself a few more kids, pastor."

Maybe he unwittingly had.

"What do you think, Casey? Do you want a rabbit?"

She stared at the little creatures, grimacing.

"I think they're defective. They don't have any hair."

"Give them a day or two. They're still brand new."

"From hev'n," Amy said.

"That's right, Amy. From heaven." Stephen reached out to ruffle Amy's head. "Babies are the Lord's way of telling us He still has hope for the future."

"Amen," Bert assented as he attached the bottle to the cage.

Casey didn't know how to respond—but blast her hormones! If she didn't get out of here quick, she was going to cry.

Spinning on her toe, she tried to escape, but Stephen's voice caught her midway.

"Casey, I need to talk to you about—"

She had to get out of here. Now. Before he saw her blubber.

To her infinite relief, the phone rang. But even as

she hurried out of the room to answer it, she knew she couldn't dodge the man for long.

He wanted to talk to her.

Had he somehow discovered her secret? she wondered as she raced down the stairs. Was he going to pull her into his office and...

Counsel her?

Fire her?

"Rectory," she panted as she ran to Stephen's desk and grabbed the receiver.

"Casey, is that you?"

Casey frowned, then realized that Erica was on the other end of the line.

"Oh, Erica," she sobbed, shutting the door with her foot and sinking into Stephen's chair. "I'm so glad you called."

"Why? What's wrong?" Erica's concern was liberally laced with professional determination and calm.

"Oh, Erica," Casey sobbed again. "I think I'm falling in love."

Chapter Eight

Casey leaned against the rough wooden railing of the porch and breathed deeply of the night air.

Erica had done her best to calm Casey's attack of emotionalism. But even now, days later, Casey couldn't banish her sense of want. Need.

Why couldn't she have the pastor for herself? It wasn't as if he were married.

But then she heard a bump, a squeal, and knew she had five very good reasons. Seven if she wanted to count the twins. Fifteen if she wanted to include the rabbits.

"There are too many people in this house," she muttered.

"What?"

Myrtle's shout caused her to shoot a look over her shoulder as Myrtle and Anne appeared on the other side of the screen.

"We're on our way to the Beckers'," Anne announced, brushing past Myrtle, who had paused midway through the door. "Way Out Widow-Maker has a match against Sven the Svelte and we can't miss it. I'm sure you understand.''

Anne handed Myrtle an enormous plastic container of popcorn and fumbled in her purse for her keys. ''Bert! Shake a leg!'' she shouted as she finally located the jingling ring.

''Have a good time,'' Casey called as the troop marched toward Anne's enormous car and squeezed into the front seat.

''We will,'' Anne confidently replied as she opened her door. With one foot inside, she leveled a finger in Casey's direction. ''Be good,'' she advised.

Casey wasn't sure, but she thought the old woman winked at her.

The car backed up, then roared away—and Casey was quite sure she caught Bert grinning slyly.

Those devils. They were matchmaking!

Laughing to herself, Casey felt the tension of the day ebb from her limbs and the rush of awkward emotions coalesce into a radiant sense of peace.

Ruckerville had proved to be so different from what she'd expected. The people were open and supportive, the farmland beautiful. Here, true pleasures were cherished and fostered—friendship, love, commitment.

Could anyone's existence really get any better than this? Casey thought with wonder. She hadn't realized how her life-style in New York had tuned her body and mind to a frantic pace. She'd always been rushing somewhere—to the subway, to the radio station, to her apartment for a few hours of sleep.

Yet, here in Ruckerville, as she breathed deeply of the scents of freshly cut hay and stared up at the brilliant pinpricks of the stars, she felt parts of her relaxing from an inner tension she hadn't even known she'd been harboring.

"Something wrong?"

A shot of pleasure shot through her system when Stephen's soft voice came to her from the house. Glancing over her shoulder, she saw his body silhouetted behind the screen, his hips cocked, his arms braced against the wooden frame. The stance merely heightened her awareness of his athletic strength and the way he made her body tingle with her own heightened sensuality.

"Not at all. I was just enjoying the quiet."

He laughed. "I take it you didn't hear the screams of discontent from the troops."

"No. Why were they discontented?"

"I refused to read *The Cat in the Hat* more than seven times." His voice was wry as he pushed through the screen and joined her. "I think I've got it memorized by now."

"Wait until they discover *Hop on Pop.*"

"I dread the day. Thank goodness they all fell asleep."

Turning, Casey leaned against the newel post and studied the man who was becoming much more than her employer. The rapport they had always shared had only deepened over the past few weeks, and there was no denying their mutual interest in each other.

But, until tonight, Casey hadn't realized how others were beginning to pick up on the silent vibrations. Their attraction had been noted by Anne, Bert and Myrtle. And judging by the way their elderly housemates had given them time alone, not everyone was opposed to an outsider capturing the minister's attention.

If only Casey was free to indulge in the experience. She would give almost anything to bask in the heated regard of his eyes, to snatch stolen moments alone together. He made her feel so alive, so beautiful. Never, in all her life, would she have thought that a man could be so...so...

Sexy?

Arousing?

Abruptly straightening, Casey returned her attention to the stars.

Get a grip on yourself.

"I'm always amazed at how black the sky is at night here in Ruckerville."

"That's because there are no city lights to compete with the stars."

A comfortable silence spooled between them before she admitted, "I never would have dreamed Kansas could be so lovely."

"What did you expect?"

She thought a moment before saying, "Something in black and white, I suppose."

His brow lifted. "Black and white?"

"Oh, come on," she teased. "Even a minister has to have seen *The Wizard of Oz* a dozen times. As a child, I used to scrunch in front of the television with my eyes closed during the portion with the tornado. Then, once it was over, I'd watch very carefully for that exact instant when the whole screen flooded with color.''

Stephen eyed her with something akin to wonder. "I have no idea what you're talking about. I've never seen *The Wizard of Oz*."

She stared at him in disbelief. "No? Really?"

"Really. I read the book once."

"As a kid?"

"No, it was part of a literature course I took in graduate school. I had to write a paper on the political allegory associated with the novel."

Casey eyed him with open suspicion, sure he was teasing her. But since he was a pastor...surely he wouldn't lie about such a thing.

"You have to get out more," she muttered.

His bark of laughter was immediate. "And you, Casey, must never, never hold back what you think."

She grimaced. "I suppose I do have a tendency for bluntness."

"And I find the quality completely refreshing."

His regard became so pointed, so intense, that she was the one who was forced to look away.

He seemed content to leave her to her own thoughts, but after several minutes inquired, "How's life in the dormitory?"

She shrugged. "Fine, I suppose."

"Is the fish adapting?"

"As well as any fish can. But Anne still won't give me a key."

He leaned down to whisper next to her ear, "Maybe she thinks you have designs on my virtue."

A rash of gooseflesh pebbled her skin, but for the life of her, she couldn't think of a thing to say to diffuse the situation. Her brain had gone completely blank, and her body was being pulled irretrievably toward the man at her side.

"Then again, maybe she's been reading *my* mind," he added in a voice that slid through her body in a velvet caress.

Her toes curled in her shoes and a frisson of excitement burst through her veins.

"I thought you told me abstinence was part of your job description," she said breathlessly.

"It is. But even a minister can be tempted."

A groan lodged in her throat, but to her relief, he didn't pull her into his arms. Instead, one fingertip slid from her temple to her jaw.

Quivering, she closed her eyes, knowing that the time had come to put a stop to the sensual undertones. If she didn't, she wouldn't be able to stop the evening from leading them both to the brink of surrender.

"Don't," she whispered.

She wasn't sure if he heard her. His finger hovered next to the corner of her mouth—and she knew that if she shifted a fraction of an inch…

She heard Stephen breathe deeply of the night air. Then to her relief and her infinite disappointment, he lowered his hand and put a few inches of space between them.

"That's part of the reason why I thought I should talk to you tonight."

"What?" she said distractedly. She couldn't even remember what they'd been talking about.

"The dormitory."

"Oh?"

"I've been thinking about the situation for some time."

Situation? What situation? Was he talking about the women who shared the wing with her? Casey's need of a key?

Or had his thoughts strayed to more dangerous areas? Such as her precarious virtue?

Or his.

"You've been here over a month now, so you've had time to grow accustomed to how my days rarely progress as planned. Even so, you've managed to be an enormous help to me."

A warmth spread through her body at the compliment.

"Nevertheless, I'm sure you'll be wanting some privacy—especially in light of the recent...additions to the rectory."

Finally, Casey understood the gist of his conversation. Stephen was worried that she was uncomfortable with her living arrangements at the rectory.

How could she tell him that such a thought hadn't entered her mind? That she'd grown to love living in the same building as Stephen Dubois?

"I've thought about the idea for a few days and had something of a brainstorm. I'll show you, if you want."

What did she want?

She couldn't think. She could barely breathe.

But she finally managed to croak, "Sure."

With a wave of his hand, Stephen gestured for her to precede him down the steps.

"You first," she said instead.

Casey had hoped that by having Stephen take the lead she would have a few moments to compose herself and still her racing heart. But by following him, she was confronted with the very appealing sight of Stephen's thick hair curling over his collar, the cling of his sweatshirt to muscular shoulders, and a tight, athletic derriere in a pair of worn jeans.

You're out of control, Casey.

Even the stern inner voice of warning couldn't drag her gaze away. She'd confessed to Erica that she thought she was falling in love with Stephen Dubois. But she feared that such a momentous event had already taken place.

No. Not now. Pregnant women didn't fall in love.

"Here we are."

Casey blinked. She'd been so absorbed with her "view" that she hadn't been paying attention to where they were going. Looking up, she realized they'd stopped in front of the wide garage with its old-fashioned doors.

Her brow furrowed as she asked, "You want me to live in the garage?"

"No, silly."

Now, why did that indulgent reprimand sound like an endearment?

He took her hand and led her up the wooden staircase that led to the second floor. Swinging the door open, he gestured to the wide, airless space that had obviously doubled as a storage area. The floor was crowded with boxes and crates and miscellaneous junk.

"I came in earlier to look around, and there are water hookups in the far corner there. With the help of some parishioners, it shouldn't be too difficult to frame in a bathroom and a small kitchen—even a bedroom, if you like. Or, if you want to keep the space open and airy, we could install the major appliances in a set of islands here and here." He pulled her through the maze of crates, pointing to the spots he'd envisioned.

Casey was immediately intrigued by the idea. One wall of the upper garage was almost entirely made of multipaned windows. The ceilings were high and vaulted, and the floor beneath her feet was scuffed but clearly hardwood. With a little work, the entire area could make a stunning loft-style apartment.

"Well? What do you think?"

Still holding her hand in his own, Stephen led her in a wandering circle—from the water hookups in the corner, to the wall of windows, then back to the door.

Judging by Stephen's expression, he was clearly enthused by the idea. "With a little hard work and some fresh paint, we should have a very comfortable apartment ready for you—probably in less than a month. That way you can come and go as you please.''

"And you? Will you be coming and going?" The moment the words left her mouth, she wished she hadn't uttered them.

But the flare in his eyes soon convinced her otherwise. Evidently, she hadn't been mistaken in her conclusion that the powerful sexual attraction between them was mutual.

"That depends," he said slowly, closing the distance that remained in such minute increments, she longed to grab him by the shirt and yank him against her.

"On what?" her voice took on a breathy quality that she didn't recognize in herself.

"Is that what you want? For me to come and go? From your apartment?"

"I…"

He shook his head, grimacing. "Perhaps you shouldn't answer that."

"On the grounds it might incriminate me?" she asked ruefully.

"No. On the grounds that it might incriminate us both."

The warmth of his gaze grew into a smolder of something she could only identify as…desire?

He cupped her cheek in his palm, and she nearly melted beneath the caress. She was so hungry for him that she gravitated toward him like a flower to the sun. Her body had grown so finely tuned to his presence, that even now, she trembled in pleasure from the simple contact.

Licking her lips, she forced her desire back. There were so many obstacles to a relationship between them—stumbling blocks that she should have had the courage to point out long ago.

"Before you commit yourself to anything, Pastor, I think you should know that I've never played by your rules before."

His brow creased. "What do you mean?"

She bit her lip, wondering how to respond without tainting herself in his eyes.

"I've never...dated a minister before."

"Is that what we're contemplating? Dating me?"

Had she assumed too much? she thought frantically. But the brush of his thumb across her lips left her in no doubt that he wasn't opposed to the idea.

"I don't know what I'd call it."

"It?"

"This..."

"This overwhelming need to be near you?" he whispered, causing her stomach to clench invitingly. "The hunger for your closeness, your laughter, your cockeyed optimism. Sometimes, I wonder how I survived without it all these years."

A portion of her thrilled at his words, admitting that she had been looking for this sort of man all her life. One who wasn't afraid to open up, to give as well as receive.

"I—I suppose it's strange..."

"Darned strange."

"After all, you're a minister—"

He frowned. "You keep harping on that point, as if my position prevents me from being a man."

"No, I—"

But she knew that the title was not as simple as any other person's occupation. It wasn't merely what he did. It was who he was, what he believed, how he dreamed.

"Haven't you ever wondered why I'm one of the few single ministers in my line of work?"

She wished that she could laugh and make a joke of his comment. But the answer was suddenly of monumental importance to her.

"Yes."

He inched closer, his body bumping against her own, reminding her that even as an expectant mother, she was still a woman. A woman who had yearnings of her own, desires...

Fears.

He traced the line of her jaw with his knuckle, and she shivered from the tenderness in that single gesture.

"I have been encouraged to marry on several occasions." His laugh held a note of bitterness. "Folks in this town would like nothing better than to see me married—especially to one of their beautiful young ladies."

She could barely breathe at his mention of other women. He was the catch of Ruckerville, everyone knew that.

So why did the thought of the parade of women inspire such a primal wave of jealousy?

"But I take my life as seriously as I take my calling, Casey." His fingers tangled in her hair, causing her to look at him. "I've seen the results of unhappy marriages and rushed decisions firsthand—as a counselor and as the son of such star-crossed lovers. My brother and I were well loved, our needs were met, and we are happy, fully adjusted adults. But that doesn't mean that I would willfully impose the pain of a dissolving relationship on anyone, let alone my own children. So I've always held myself back, knowing that if I waited long enough, my other half would cross my path."

Her chest tightened as he took her hand and set it over his heart.

"You see, I believe in soul mates and happily-ever-afters. I know, I know. Such views are incredibly impractical and idealistic for a man who has made it his life's work to serve others."

Casey felt like crying. How, after all these years, could she have found such a modern miracle, a man who believed in commitment, service, compassion...

And true love.

"I always thought that when I found a woman who shared all those same ideals and dreams, I would take things slow. I'd woo her with all the leisurely grace that our modern world frowns upon. I would remember that part of happiness is the pursuit, and the most powerful aphrodisiac is an unassuaged desire. But for the life of me, I can't seem to slow down when you're near.''

Her eyes closed at the poetry of his words, the uncommon frankness, the sheer beauty.

Then her eyes stung with unshed tears as she realized that Stephen was not for her. She had already surrendered her rights to such a man. After all the time that had passed, how could she inform him that the very miracle—*miracles*—that had brought them together would eventually keep them apart?

Her babies.

Breaking away from him, she burst from the storage room and moved onto the landing. Gripping the rough railing, she gulped air into her lungs to push away the dizziness that threatened to consume her.

But Stephen didn't give her much time to think of something to say. Instead, he cupped her shoulders with his hands, pulling her back against his chest.

"Don't be afraid, Casey. I would never hurt you. Not for this world."

But had she hurt him? Had she unconsciously flirted with disaster if only to be able to say that she had once known a man like Stephen Dubois?

"Will you let me court you, Casey?"

She searched frantically for the right thing to say, finally settling on, "It's so soon. We've only known each other a little while."

"Time is relative when something feels right. And this—*you*, feel so right in my arms."

His hands slid down to her elbows, wrists, then

one arm curled around her chest and he rested his chin on her shoulder.

"Your congregation…"

"I'm here to help them, Casey, to guide them, to serve them. But I can no more live my life through them than they can through me."

"They'll talk…"

"Gossip is part of small-town life but is generally harmless."

"I don't want to tarnish your reputation."

He laughed, the sound husky and sensual. "Once again, I'm confronted with the fact that you evidently have some mistaken impression that I'm a saint or an angel."

Turning her in his embrace, he tipped her chin as his head dipped. "I'm neither, Casey. I'm a man, through and through. I've made mistakes and committed my share of sins. But there could be no sin in loving you. Not when God has answered my prayers and brought you to me."

She blinked at the tears that sprang to her eyes. "I'm not a religious person, Stephen."

"Says who?"

"I'm not kind and meek and mild."

"You sound as if you're describing a sheep."

"No. A minister's…wi—" Not wife. He hadn't proposed, and she mustn't assume that he ever would. Not when such a step would involve rearing seven children under the age of three.

Seven.

"I'm not the sort of person who could be a minister's...companion."

"Is that what you are? My companion?"

"No, I..."

He set a finger over her lips. "Somehow you've bought into the Hollywood stereotype of what being a pastor means. How many times do I have to tell you, Casey? I'm a man. I'm just a man."

Then he was kissing her, filling her with his strength and his passion.

She moaned against him, clinging to him for support, knowing that there was no other place on earth that she would rather be than here. With him.

Breaking free, she wound her arms around his neck and hugged him tightly to her, praying that she wasn't making a mistake in indulging in this one selfish moment. But she knew that as soon as he discovered that she was pregnant—not as a result of a loving union, but as a product of modern technology—he would never look at her the same way. He would never hold her as if she were a treasure on earth. He would never woo her at all.

Nevertheless, when he held her close, her heart pounded in her chest and a warmth settled low in her belly, reminding her that just as he had asserted that he was nothing more than a man, she was only a woman. She didn't have the superhuman resolve that would be necessary to refuse the temptation offered by Stephen's arms. She wanted to revel in his passion. She wanted to sate her own desires and forget about all the worries the future would bring.

"Stephen, I—"

The words stuck in her throat when Casey suddenly became aware of a slight flutter deep in her body.

The sensation was so startling, so unexpected, that she broke free, thinking she'd imagined the movement. But as she held her breath, the tiny butterfly-like stirrings occurred again.

One of her babies had moved.

She gazed up at Stephen, her eyes widening in wonder and joy. But even as her lips parted to share the news with him, she realized she couldn't.

"What's wrong?"

"Nothing, I—"

Again, she turned away, plunging her hands into the pockets of her loose jumper. At a loss as to how to proceed, she pressed her hand to her stomach again, silently willing her babies to tell her what to do.

And as if by magic, she felt the fluttering again.

Immediately, she was flooded with a protectiveness that astounded her. These were *her* babies. *Her* children. *Her* twins. Suddenly, they weren't just dots on a screen or a bizarre hormonal imbalance that had the ability to turn a home pregnancy test a brilliant blue. They were living beings with growing hearts and minds. In no time at all, they would be entering this world. Within months, they would have dreams of their own to build.

And Casey wanted nothing more than to give them the world.

For the first time, she saw how her life to this point had been completely egocentric. Every decision she'd made had been for her good.

But she couldn't think like that anymore. She owed her children the best that she could give them. And just as Stephen had carefully waited for a woman who could inspire a life of happily-ever-afters, she had to see to it that every choice she made was not only good for her, but for her…

Sons?

Daughters?

Perhaps a daughter and a son?

A distant crash inside the rectory was followed by Amy's shout and Ellie's wail.

"Damn," Stephen muttered. "I thought they were asleep."

Casey tried to smile, then offered him one of her customary quips. "Maybe they're still waiting for your reprise of *The Cat in the Hat.*"

Stephen groaned. "I will not read that book again tonight." But his tone was indulgent and tinged with a thread of wonder.

He was bonding with them, Casey realized. Just as the butterfly-like movements in her womb had cemented the reality of her own children, each day that passed and each brush with the quintuplets' mischief merely solidified Stephen's role in their lives. He was becoming their father.

Idly, Casey wondered how much longer it would be before Stephen admitted what everyone in Ruckerville had already surmised. Stephen's foster sister would not be returning to collect the toddlers. She'd had two years to form emotional ties with her stepchildren.

No, Stephen was their family now. And he'd already begun to love them, deeply, completely.

He was their father.

He would always be their father.

So how could Casey demand more of him? Those children needed his strength and security. They deserved that much.

Sensing her jumbled thoughts, Stephen tenderly kissed the top of her head.

"Think about what I've said," he whispered. "And for heaven's sake, don't deify me because of my position in this community. I've got to fall head over heels for a woman sometime, you know. You just happen to be the perfect candidate."

As his footsteps disappeared behind her, Casey squeezed her eyes shut, praying that she wouldn't cry. Not here. Not now.

Why did she have to be so irresistible? she asked herself, then burst into laughter at her own conceit.

Wiping the moisture from her cheeks, Casey damned the rollicking emotions inspired by her pregnancy. She had to think. Think!

Stephen had all but admitted he was falling in love with her. She couldn't allow herself to regard the phenomenon as a tragedy. But she couldn't allow such a thing to happen, either. For both their sakes, she needed to bring this romance to a halt and return their relationship to a professional footing.

So what was she going to do?

Pushing her shoulders back, she marched down the stairs, her resolve growing stronger with each step.

The minister found her irresistible. He'd all but said as much. But Casey was a resourceful, creative woman with a doctorate in psychology and an arsenal of feminine wiles at her beck and call.

By heaven, she was more than capable of discouraging his attentions. She'd show him her worst vices, her most disgusting habits—and, if need be, she'd invent a few new ones. She'd have that man so afraid of the bitter old crab she could become that he'd be locking her in the dormitory himself.

Moreover, she would make him think the whole change of heart was his idea. Then, when she told him of her condition, he'd consider himself lucky to be rid of her.

Chapter Nine

In the end, Casey delayed her campaign to "disinterest" the pastor by looking for a house of her own. As convenient as it might be to live over the garage in the apartment Stephen had told her about, she knew that such an option was out of the question. With temptation so close, she would be bound to succumb sooner or later.

Calling upon one of the local real estate agents, she made a tour of the available properties—from farmhouses to Ruckerville's newest subdivision. But it was while she was touring a stately Queen Anne that she discovered "the nursery"—a tiny room off the master bedroom that had been formed from the octagonal shape of the house's turret. Immediately, she envisioned the walls covered in pretty paper, net curtains, two frilly bassinets, two stately cribs.

"I'll take it," she said to the elegantly coiffed Realtor.

"But don't you want to see the rest of the house?"

"No. Just give me the name of a few structural

engineers or contractors I can bring in to examine things. I want to make sure it's in relatively good shape before I totally commit to the project. But if everything is in order, I should have an offer ready by the end of the week.''

"Wonderful!"

And the situation *was* wonderful. A local contractor had taken Casey on a tour of the house, pointing out the recent rewiring, the soundness of the hardwood subfloors, the high-grade shingles installed only three years earlier. He was also completely candid about the need to replace the cracked front steps, reseal the concrete porch and install double-paned windows.

But when his estimates were totaled, her mortgage approved and her offer accepted, she found herself the owner of her own home.

Hers.

Hers and her babies'.

"I guess that means you've decided to live in Ruckerville for a while," Erica said when Casey told her the news.

Casey hadn't even admitted as much to herself. Her decision had been made on "emotional autopilot," and at those odd times when she'd paused long enough to ponder making such a long-lasting commitment, she'd told herself that she'd merely felt it best to get away from the rectory. Moreover, it was wiser to buy than to rent.

But the truth of the matter was, she loved living in Ruckerville. In the few weeks she'd been here, she'd bonded with the people, slid comfortably into the slower-paced life-style and become addicted to waking up to birdsong.

"I like it here," she said simply.

"I'm glad."

"I've already talked to my agent. With my show going into syndication, the powers-that-be at WMMN have agreed to pool efforts with the local country-and-western station. WMMN will update their recording equipment in exchange for my unlimited use of their facilities. There's even talk of the local group merging with the parent broadcasting company."

"Fantastic."

"I've also been approached about writing a book and submitting a regular column to the *Illinois Register.*"

"My, my. Your leave of absence seems to have given your career a boost."

"Thanks to the loyal fans who've been demanding my return."

"So I guess you're set."

"Hmm."

But as she and Erica moved on to other topics, Casey knew that—as wonderful as all the changes might be—she would miss living in the rectory.

Just as she would miss living with the minister.

WHEN THE TIME CAME to break the news of her imminent relocation to Stephen, Casey's stomach became such a tangle of butterflies, she thought she would embarrass herself by being sick.

But, taking a deep breath, she marched determinedly to Stephen's office. Before she walked out the door again, she intended to tell him about the house *and* the twins.

"Pastor, I—"

The words locked in her throat when she skidded to a halt and discovered Stephen sprawled on the leather couch, five towheaded girls sprawled against him, sleeping.

Had he stayed up with them all night again?

Since Stephen had confessed to her that the quintuplets seemed to have permanently regulated their bodies to time in India, she'd suggested reading to them in the hopes of helping them sleep when they woke at one or two in the morning. He must have taken her advice, because he'd spent the better part of the wee hours reading…

Hop on Pop.

She snickered. She'd warned him about the book, about the repetitious words that enthralled youngsters but sent adults careering toward the brink of madness. He should have taken her advice.

A little body stirred, and a pair of bright eyes blinked and focused. Then, the most beautiful, heart-tugging smile Casey had ever seen spread over the face of one of the toddlers.

"Mama?" she asked sleepily.

Casey nearly burst into tears. *Mama.*

Reluctantly, she shook her head, recognizing the quintuplet as being Ellie—the one hungry for love.

"No, sweetheart. I'm not your mama."

Bending, Casey scooped Ellie from the tangle of arms and legs. But in doing so, the other children started as if a bomb had exploded.

"Shh," Casey whispered. "Let's go get you some breakfast, hmm?"

Still sleepy and uncoordinated, the toddlers wriggled off the couch and headed in the direction of the kitchen. Casey tiptoed after them, but she'd only gone as far as the doorway when a gruff voice inquired, "Casey?"

She turned and smiled, then curled her toes in her shoes to keep from running to him, thrusting her fingers through his hair and demanding a kiss.

This is what it would be like to wake up to Stephen, a little voice whispered.

No. She couldn't think about that. She couldn't think about his rumpled hair, stubble-darkened chin, or the way he languidly stretched his arms over his head and yawned.

How could something so mundane be so completely erotic?

"Good morning." Her voice was garbled with her efforts to keep the desire from her tone.

He settled back into place and eyed her through heavy lashes.

"Where are the rest of the rug rats?" he asked indulgently.

"On their way to the kitchen."

Stephen yawned again. "I'll make waffles."

His eyes were growing heavier, and she said, "You don't have to do that. I can fix them something."

"No. It's time I made you some waffles, too. Especially since you'll be moving soon."

Her stomach flip-flopped. Damn. She'd forgotten about the speed of the town grapevine.

She must have looked stricken, because he grinned. "The old Benson place is a wonderful house—and you're getting a good buy."

"Then you're not mad about my not accepting the apartment over the garage?"

He shook his head. "Actually, I found the fact that you'd buy a house a very promising sign."

Again, her stomach jumped, but this time from something far more sensual.

"Why is that?"

"It sounds to me like you're putting down roots."

"I suppose so."

"That means you won't be going anywhere soon."

She licked her lips.

"No. I suppose not."

"Good. I'll be able to court you properly, then."

Tell him. Tell him about the twins.

His eyes warmed. "This way, I won't cause as much gossip when I try to send you flowers. Having a different address will help matters immensely."

Tell him. Tell him now. You already can't fit into

*a pair of trousers; within another week or two, you'll
be big as a whale.*

"In fact, I got to thinking that I'll still refurbish
the garage apartment. It has nearly twelve-hundred
square feet. I thought I'd offer it to Anne, Myrtle and
Bert."

Why did such a simple announcement make her
heart pound and her throat go dry? But then again,
maybe it had nothing to do with her announcement
and everything to do with the way he was looking at
her.

Like a man...

In love?

No. They were still little more than strangers.

But she couldn't deny there was some severe
"like" gleaming in his indigo eyes.

Ellie tugged on Casey's collar.

"Bek-fast," she reminded Casey.

Casey had to forcefully wrench her mind back to
the little girl in her arms.

"Yes. Breakfast," she echoed weakly.

Stephen swung his feet to the floor and rose from
the couch in one lithe movement. As he did so, she
discovered that the crocheted afghan he'd thrown
over his legs had not hidden a full pair of sweatpants
as she'd assumed. Instead, the soft cloth had been
cut away somewhere at mid-thigh to expose his taut
muscles and hair-dusted skin.

*Please, please, don't let me succumb to temptation
now.*

As if sensing at least a portion of her thoughts,

Stephen paused in front of her, then took her chin in a gentle grip. Leaning over the baby, he offered Casey a kiss that was slow, sweet and oh, so addicting.

She couldn't seem to catch her breath when he backed away.

"I'll just shower and meet you in the kitchen."

He could have told her to meet him on the moon and she would have found a way to obey him.

"Yes, sir."

He chuckled, then scooped Ellie out of her arms. "Come on, little girl. You're getting much too big for anyone to be carrying you, but I'll let it go this time. After all, you're my snookums, aren't you?"

He was walking down the hall, but Casey clearly heard Ellie say, "Papa?"

There was a moment's pause, then he said, "I suppose I am. At least for a little while."

"Papa."

Casey heard the thunder of feet, then Stephen's "Come on, everybody. I'll race you upstairs. Grace is up there changing your sheets and you can help," he said, referring to their baby-sitter, Grace Smith.

Amid the squeals and thumping footfalls, Casey laid her hands on her stomach.

Stephen was a brave, brave man. He had accepted the responsibility of caring for the community, three elderly parishioners, quintuplets, Casey…

And your twins?

She shouldn't be afraid of telling him the truth.

So why don't you?

Because he'll…

He'll what? Faint?

No, she realized, heartsick and filled with self-pity. *He won't send me flowers.*

CASEY GAVE THE CONTRACTOR free rein with the Queen Anne under the stipulation that the changes and repairs she'd authorized would be finished within two weeks.

Then she began—in earnest—her campaign to repel Stephen Dubois.

If she could get him to realize that he was better off without her, life would be so much easier. She would be able to continue as his assistant without any awkwardness. Their relationship would become one of professionals, with only a hint of friendship. Then she would be able to forget that she had ever been attracted to the man.

You're pitiful.

Step one in her agenda was to let Stephen Dubois see what she was really like in the morning. She didn't comb her hair, apply makeup or censure her attire. Instead, she stumbled down to breakfast in her enormous ratty robe and slippers shaped like bear paws.

But when Stephen whispered in her ear one day how "adorable" she looked, she knew she had to try harder.

Concentrating on all of the annoying habits she'd ever heard being discussed by other women and their husbands, she drank milk from the carton, left the peanut butter jar on the cabinet, crunched noisily on ice and began carrying a forty-four-ounce Big Sip everywhere she went.

To her disappointment, the only real effect of her vices was an increased amount of quality bathroom time.

Digging into the heavy artillery, she flossed in public, complained about her mother's sciatica, ran up long-distance phone calls to Erica and even belched once without excusing herself.

So what was she supposed to do now? Pierce her nose and write dirty haikus in the church lavatories?

"You look very pensive."

Casey jumped when Stephen suddenly spoke from behind her shoulder. Planting a hand on her rapidly beating chest, she gasped, "Don't *do* that!"

"Do what?"

"Sneak up on me."

"I called your name three times."

"Oh."

Casey knew that at this point she should wipe her nose on her sleeve, curse or scratch. But frankly, she didn't have the heart. She would simply have to accept the fact that she was irresistible and nothing would ever change that quality.

Yeah, right.

Doing her best to ignore the erratic beating of her heart, she returned to her task, deadheading the rose-bushes and searching for the choicest blooms.

"Where are the girls?" she asked, peering around his shoulder.

"Asleep. It's nap time." The comment was rife with enjoyment.

"Count your lucky stars they went down at the same time."

"I have already cataloged and reviewed the blessings involved, thank you."

"You seem in bright spirits today."

"Haven't you heard? The church picnic social is scheduled two weeks from this Saturday." He extended a daisy in her direction, despite the fact that she held a basket of blossoms she'd been cutting for the chapel.

"Why, thank you."

"You're welcome." He inched closer and dipped his head to whisper in her ear. "I also came to ask you to accompany me."

"On errands?"

"No, silly. To the picnic." He brushed a lock of hair from her brow, the movement completely unconscious and rife with intimacy.

Her brows raised. "You're asking me two weeks in advance?"

"I wouldn't want anyone to beat me to the opportunity."

"And you want *me* to be your date?"

"Of course."

"Isn't that dangerous?"

"Do you bite?"

"No, but I would think a pastor would want to keep his personal life...personal."

"I don't plan to neck with you under the bridge, I'm just taking you on a date."

A date. How could such an innocent-sounding title be so rife with sensual undertones?

"Nola Wilkens will be shocked."

"Nola Wilkens needs to lighten up."

"What about your reputation?"

He pretended to be shocked. "Are you an ax murderer?"

"No."

"A bordello madam?"

"No."

"An embezzler on the lam?"

"No."

"Then I don't see what you can possibly do to my reputation."

"But I thought you were supposed to be a symbol of all that's right and good in the world."

"So what's not right and good about a man and a woman being attracted to each other?"

"I…"

He grinned. "I'm beginning to believe that you're the one who needs to loosen up."

"I do not! I'll have you know that in New York, I had a wild reputation."

"Ahh. Casey Fairchild, the shock jock of WMMN."

She gaped at him. "You knew that was me?"

"Of course. I heard you several times while I was at a conference in Manhattan. I recognized your voice the first time we met." His tone dropped, becoming more suggestive. "That night when you stopped me on the street—"

"I was waiting at an intersection."

"Gave me your come-hither look—"

"I was trying to start my car."

"Then said, 'Take me home, you awesome hunk of man.'"

She burst out laughing. "You really have a high opinion of yourself, don't you?"

"I try my best. Will you come to the picnic with me?"

She hesitated.

"We'll have five little chaperones."

Phrased that way, what could possibly happen to make the engagement anything but platonic?

It could be done.

No. Nothing must happen between them. She'd waited so long in telling Stephen about the twins that she'd outgrown her jeans *and* elastic waistbands. The moment he touched her stomach...

She nearly groaned aloud in anxiety. Perhaps the picnic would be the perfect place to make such a confession. There would be lots of people and distractions. If she could manage to pull Stephen to one side, she could inform him of her condition. Then, with his congregation surrounding him, he couldn't yell at her.

Not that she thought he'd yell, but...

He might curse.

And his parishioners would prevent him from sinning any more in her presence than he'd already done.

"Hey, Pastor!" A voice shouted from the door of the main building. "We're all here and you promised to help us with our merit badges."

"I'll take your silence as a yes," Stephen said softly, touching his finger to her lips. "Don't worry about lunch. I'll pack everything we need."

Sighing, Casey watched Stephen bound away, heading toward the Scouting group that was scheduled to meet in the cultural hall. His carefree whistle floated through the air. He seemed so happy, so unaware of what was about to hit him right between the eyes.

Poor man.

Poor, poor man.

He was smitten with her, and no matter how much pleasure—and amazement—she derived from the fact, she knew the shock that awaited him as soon as she screwed up enough courage to blurt out the truth.

Say, Pastor, did you know you weren't dating one person, but one and two-thirds?

The thought inspired a very unladylike snort.

Go ahead, laugh it up. But no minister—no matter how young, handsome and smitten—will ever condone the unorthodox method you used to obtain those little beings hidden under your heart.

"I don't care what he thinks," she muttered out loud to herself.

But she did care. More than she ever thought she would.

Chapter Ten

The picnic was only two weeks away when Casey received a call from Erica announcing she was in town. Despite Casey's insistence that it was impractical for Erica to continue to serve as Casey's doctor while she was in Kansas, Erica had insisted.

"After all, I've got the money and I'll make the time. I plan to see this pregnancy through to the end," Erica had insisted.

Although Casey suspected that tales of Pastor Dubois had prompted the visit as much as prenatal care, she didn't argue. Right now, she needed a friend as much as she needed a physician.

"I'm in here!" Erica called when the bell over the door of the Ruckerville Clinic jingled to announce Casey's arrival.

Cautiously, Casey peered at the empty waiting room and the gleaming front desk, but just as Erica had promised, the part-time facilities were closed for the day.

Following the direction of Erica's voice, Casey

made her way to the examination rooms, shaking her head in wonder. "How in the world did you manage to get the use of this place?"

"Dr. Rob takes Wednesdays off for his weekly fishing excursion. I called and mentioned that I was coming to town to visit an old friend and we were looking for someplace quiet and private to discuss some treatments. He offered his office before I had a chance to work up to the request."

Casey shook her head. "You're a wonder."

Erica grinned. "Yes. I am."

Leaning her shoulder against the doorjamb, Casey waited as Erica readied the ultrasound equipment, her stomach clenching with nerves, her heart pounding. Although her pregnancy was a reality and the growth of her babies right on schedule, the machines still brought to mind memories of disappointment and heartache.

"Relax, Casey," Erica said without turning. "You're proceeding on schedule—even gaining a little more weight than I'd expected."

"Gee, thanks."

"Twins can play havoc on the figure. Trust me."

Finally, Erica pronounced everything ready and turned to give Casey her full attention. Her dark brows furrowed. "You don't look pregnant."

"It's all a matter of camouflage." Casey pulled the soft challis of her jumper against her stomach, revealing the burgeoning swell.

Erica beamed in delight. "There are my little twins!"

"Not so little," Casey grumbled as she took her place behind the changing screen to disrobe and don the paper gown that waited for her.

"Erica, I'm only four-and-a-half months along and I can't even fit into drawstring pants anymore."

"Big deal."

Casey poked her head around the edge of the screen. "It *is* a big deal. I only have three loose dresses."

"So I'll treat you to a trip to the big city this afternoon. After a month in Ruckerville, I bet you're dying for some fast food. We'll find something decadent to eat, shatter all our guidelines of fat content and good nutrition, then take you shopping for some maternity clothes."

"Maternity clothes!" Casey hissed in disbelief, dodging from her hiding place. "I can't wear maternity clothes!"

Erica's brows climbed. "Honey, you're expecting twins. I don't think you're going to have a choice."

"But...but then everyone will *know*."

"Know what?"

"That I'm...pregnant."

It took several seconds for Casey's pronouncement to sink into Erica's brain, then, glancing over each shoulder as if Dr. Rob might have hidden spies in the room, she demanded, "You mean you *still* haven't told anyone you're pregnant?"

"No."

"Not even Pastor Dubois?"

"No!"

Erica's face mirrored her disbelief, then her patent amusement. "Honey, I don't think you can keep your condition an indefinite secret."

"I know that," Casey retorted. "But I just couldn't…I haven't…"

Marching to the examination table, Casey climbed onto the crackling paper and clutched the gown at her chest.

Erica tipped her head. "I thought the whole point of your coming to Ruckerville was so that you could relax and enjoy the arrival of your babies."

"Dammit, Erica, I'm well aware of the reasons for my being here. It's just that…I couldn't…I mean I would have, if…"

When she began to sputter again, Erica held up her hands for silence. "Hold on a minute."

Erica searched through cabinets until she found a woolly blanket. Draping it over Casey's shoulders, she left the room, then returned, wheeling the doctor's office chair laden with pillows.

"I'm sensing that today you need me as a friend more than a doctor, so we might as well make ourselves comfortable. You take the chair. It'll be better for your back. But I want your feet up. I can see already that they're swollen."

As Casey settled into the worn vinyl squabs of Dr. Rob's chair and planted her feet on the examination table, Erica disappeared, returning moments later with a tray that held two icy glasses of lemonade, a bowl of fresh cherries and a plate of cookies.

"The lemonade is stolen from Dr. Rob's refrigerator and the cherries from the tree out back, but the cookies are my mother's.''

''Her usual recipe?''

''If you can call any of my mother's baking usual.''

Mrs. Beaman was well known for her inability to follow any recipe as outlined. She invariably added a dash of this, a bit of that. She stated proudly that she made all of her food more healthy by omitting half the butter and using applesauce instead, but when she also augmented her cookies with real cream, extra raisins and nuts, double chocolate chips or a dash of liqueur, the result was more decadent than anything originally intended.

''Decisions, decisions,'' Casey murmured as she debated between triple chocolate chocolate chip, carrot or old-fashioned jumbles.

''Just take one,'' Erica said as she lifted Casey's feet, sat on the table, then began to rub Casey's arches.

''Oooh.'' Casey sighed in delight as she took a carrot cookie topped with drizzled cream cheese frosting. Closing her eyes, she reveled in the potent pleasure of homemade cookies and a foot massage.

''You know, Erica, you could charge double with your examinations if you'd add the foot rub as a routine procedure.''

''Yeah, but then the massage therapist I recommend would be out of business.''

Chewing happily on her cookie, Casey waited for

Erica to pursue the original topic of conversation, knowing she wouldn't have long to wait.

"You need to put your feet up more, Casey."

"I know. It's been hectic lately getting all my support groups going."

"I hope this arrangement hasn't metamorphosed from a part-time job to a full-time job with part-time pay."

"No. Stephen is very strict about my limiting my hours to those outlined."

"Stephen?"

"Pastor Dubois."

When a quiet settled into the room, Casey opened her eyes enough to peer through her lashes. Erica was studying her curiously.

"You call him by his first name?"

"Of course."

"Around other people?"

"He insisted."

"And does he know you're half in love with him?"

Casey choked on the cookie. "No!"

Erica nodded, thought, then asked, "So how old is this pastor?"

"Why?"

Her friend shrugged. "No reason. I'm just curious."

"I don't know."

"Guess."

"About my age."

"Oh, boy," Erica muttered under her breath.

"What?"

Her friend chose her words carefully, then asked, "Does the pastor have anything to do with the fact that you haven't told anyone you're pregnant? Are you afraid of what they will say if they discover he's dating a woman...in the family way?"

The question hit home, but Casey waved the comment aside with a negligent hand, summoning her best carefree manner. "You're being paranoid."

"Am I?"

"Well, sure. I mean—"

"Casey, it's me, remember? You don't have to put on a show for me."

The bluster rushed from Casey's manner in a gust of air. Erica was right. There was no need to keep the truth from her. She was the closest thing Casey had ever had to a sister.

"I've already told you that I'm...attracted to him," she admitted reluctantly.

"How much?"

"A lot."

"So you really are half in love with him." Erica added gently, "Maybe even...completely in love with him—and not just due to your raging hormones?"

Casey nodded miserably.

"And is he attracted to you?"

"I think so."

"How much?"

"A lot?"

Erica laughed out loud, then caught herself and

adopted a serious mien. The attempt was a failure since her eyes sparkled with mirth.

"So what does the little town of Ruckerville think about their favorite son having a thing with his new assistant?"

"We aren't having a 'thing.' The man's a minister, for heaven's sake."

"That can't possibly keep him from shooting lustful glances in your direction." Erica's eyes widened. "Does he watch you during his sermons?"

"Erica!" But Casey blushed. Despite the fact that she didn't consider herself a religious person, she had attended a handful of Stephen's sermons by now—if only to show her support of his work. The moment he'd stood in front of his congregation—not from the intimidating height of the pulpit, but from the intimate space in front of the pews, she'd been captivated. He was so passionate about his faith, about his congregation. Rather than preaching against the evils of hell and damnation as every other pastor Casey had ever heard, he seemed dedicated to uplifting his audience, giving them hope, convincing them of God's love.

Only once had he looked at Casey as he'd spoken.

That glance had shot through her like a lightning bolt.

"He *does* look at you!" Erica exclaimed.

"No. No, he doesn't."

"Mmm. That could be even more telling. What kind of kisser is he?"

Erica's change in subject was so abrupt, that Casey automatically said, "The best I've ever had."

The moment the words were uttered, Casey blushed and Erica clapped her hands in delight.

"This is so fantastic. Just think, by sending you here I may have introduced you to Mr. Right."

"No." Casey swung her feet to the ground. "Stephen Dubois is not—can not…"

But she couldn't continue. He wasn't what?

Right?

He felt right.

Safe?

How could he be anything but safe? The man was a minister. He wasn't about to involve her in a torrid affair, then dump her like yesterday's news.

Sincere?

He *was* sincere. That was what scared her the most.

"Why are you resisting what you obviously feel for him, Casey?"

"Things are…complicated between us."

"Emotionally?"

"No. Actually, I think we both would fall into a relationship quite eagerly if things were different."

"You mean the twins?"

"Ye-es." Casey wondered how to tell Erica the rest.

"Hey," Erica said softly, taking Casey's hands. "The man's a minister. It's his job to understand."

"He also believes very strongly in having a marriage first, *then* children."

"Yes, but life doesn't always work out that way. Why are you different from any other single mother who's been forced to make the best of what fate has handed her?"

"Fate didn't put me in this situation. I *chose* to be here."

"And if he's half the man you evidently think he is, Stephen Dubois will understand your reasons," Erica insisted. She waited until Casey looked at her. "You and I both know that the fact that you're pregnant at all is a miracle. If you hadn't taken matters into your own hands when you did, there's a possibility that you never would have had children."

"I know that. I just…" Casey took a deep breath. "I've tried to tell him. I honestly thought all the loose clothes would give me away by now."

Erica's eyes held hers, their concern apparent. "Casey, you've got to say something. If you wait until he figures this out on his own, he'll wonder why you didn't trust him enough to confide in him."

"I know that. But if his reaction to the twins was my only worry, then I—"

Casey broke off when an engine roared past the clinic. Instantly, her breath snagged in her throat.

Stephen's Suburban. She'd know the sound of that vehicle anywhere.

Sure enough, within seconds, there was a screech of brakes, the revving of the motor, then the Suburban pulled into the drive.

"Oh, my gosh," Casey said, scrambling to her feet. "That's him."

"Who?"

"Stephen. He must have seen my car. He was gone when you called, so I didn't have a chance to give some sort of excuse as to where I'd be going. He probably thinks I'm here for...who knows what!"

"Calm down."

"I can't calm down. He can't see me like this! I'm...pregnant!"

"No kidding," Erica said ruefully.

"This isn't funny."

"I know, I know. Relax. Get your clothes on." Erica moved to peer out of the window. "I'll stall him until you come out."

Casey ran behind the screen. Ripping the paper gown from her shoulders, she reached for her clothes.

Distantly, she could hear a squeak of the driver's door.

Erica offered a soft wolf whistle.

"My, my, my. I never had a minister who looked like *that*. Congratulations, Casey."

Casey merely moaned, searching in vain for her bra.

"Is he coming up to the clinic?"

"Yes, although...I think he has someone with him."

Casey groaned, decided to forgo the bra and fumbled to draw her shirt over her head.

"No, I take that back. He must be in charge of some sort of day care. His Suburban is chock-full of car seats. He's got at least four—"

"Five," Casey corrected her as she slipped the jumper over her head, noted it was inside out and ripped it off again, discovering her bra dangling from the front pocket in the process. "He has five car seats. And it isn't a day care."

"Then what is he doing driving around with a car full of kids?"

Casey finally managed to slip into her clothing and ran from behind the screen, searching the floor for her shoes.

"They're his kids."

Erica was completely perplexed. "His kids? I thought you said he was single."

"He is."

"He's a widower?"

"No. He's never been married. But just after I arrived, he…" Casey sighed. Then, gesturing wide to the Suburban, the toddlers and the lean man heading to the door, she said, "*That's* why I haven't been able to tell Stephen I'm pregnant with twins. Stephen has recently become the guardian of toddler quintuplets."

"I think I need a drink," Erica mumbled as the outer door opened and the bell jingled. "No. I *know* I need a drink."

"Casey?" A deep voice called from the waiting room. "Dr. Rob?"

Casey grabbed Erica's hands. "You can't tell him I'm pregnant. I'll do it myself when I can find a good time to break the news."

Erica rolled her eyes. "Honey, you aren't ever going to find a good time to break the news of twins to a man who already has quintuplets.''

''Shh!''

''Casey?''

Holding a warning finger to her lips, Casey dodged out of the room, slamming the door behind her.

Chapter Eleven

"Hi!" She winced when her voice emerged too high, too perky, too...

Guilty.

She sounded guilty as hell.

"Did you need me for something?" she asked, nervously smoothing her hair.

"No. I saw your car and..." He stared at her, and his obvious concern only increased the pounding of her heart. "Are you all right? Dr. Rob usually goes fishing on Wednesdays, so when I saw you were here, I got a little worried."

He worried about her.

The thought was so wonderful, she could have cried. But since that would only alarm him even more, she laughed instead—then wished she hadn't when she sounded slightly hysterical.

"No, no, nothing's wrong," she said, hastening to relieve him. "Actually, I had a call after you left. One of my friends arrived unexpectedly in Ruckerville. She's a doctor..."

Don't go there.

"And she was visiting a patient in Ruckerville…"

Bad move.

"Who, I don't know…"

Oh, yeah, right.

"Anyway, she called…"

You said that already.

"And invited me to lunch."

Stephen rested his knuckles on his hips, and Casey swallowed when the unconscious stance caused the fabric of his black shirt to pull taut against his chest. The white strip of his clerical collar merely enhanced the angularity of his jaw.

"You aren't going to eat here, are you?" he asked, glancing at the waiting room.

Laugh. Did she really sound as much like the village idiot as she feared she did?

"Of course not. I'm just meeting her here." She dropped her voice to a whisper. "She's just…uh… finishing an exam."

Stupid, stupid, stupid. He saw you leaping out of that room as if it were on fire.

"I was…uh…just helping."

His brow furrowed. Dammit, she was making everything worse. She was explaining too much. She should just keep her mouth shut and act casual.

"I didn't know you had any medical training."

"I don't, I just…lightbulb."

"What?"

Her hands moved in restless gestures. "One of the lightbulbs burned out and I brought E—"

Did he know Erica? They were cousins. Judging by Erica's reaction, they'd never met, but that didn't mean that Stephen hadn't heard about Erica. For all I know, he could be aware of the distant cousin who specialized in infertility.

"I just brought my friend a lightbulb."

Great. Now he probably thinks you're a blithering idiot. It's not enough that he caught you playing dolls with the unwed mothers. Now you're skulking around the local doctor's office babbling about lightbulbs.

Knowing she had to get him out of the clinic before Erica decided to emerge from her hiding place and force a confession, Casey began walking to the door. Just as she'd hoped, Stephen automatically fell into step beside her.

"You're dressed up for a Wednesday afternoon," she said, referring to the way he usually wore dark sweatshirts with his clerical collar when he worked around town.

"I'm headed for Wichita."

"Really?" She and Erica would have to choose somewhere else for fast food and maternity shopping.

"I got a package from Lexi today—"

Casey instinctively gripped his arm. "Not another baby."

He chuckled. "No. She sent a sheaf of medical documents, a long letter and a videotaped confession of sorts."

"What do you mean?"

Stephen paused at the door he'd left ajar. "She's feeling guilty about sending the quintuplets to me."

And so she should, Casey thought.

Stephen must have guessed her thoughts, because he laughed. "There's no need to look so disapproving."

"I didn't mean—"

"I know you didn't mean to, because frankly, I've been battling with my own disapproval. But in her video, Lexi was quite candid. The children were her husband's, actually. He was a widower when they married."

"This was the man she met in—"

"Kuala Lumpur," Stephen supplied.

"Kuala Lumpur," Casey echoed. She wasn't even sure she knew where that was exactly.

"Anyhow, when she married the man and they moved to India, he failed to tell her that he hoped she would be a full-time mother for his daughters. He'd begun to believe he couldn't handle them on his own."

"Gee. What was his first clue?"

"Anyway, she didn't even learn about the toddlers until she'd been married a month."

"What a great guy."

"That's what I thought."

But you haven't told Stephen about the twins, her conscience prodded.

True enough, but I'm not about to marry him and *then* spring the news.

"Anyhow, about a week after being introduced to

her new daughters, Lexi's husband was killed by a charging bull.''

Stephen leaned a hand against the wall and Casey's stomach flip-flopped with sensual awareness.

Someone should tell him that what he did to a pair of jeans and a cotton dress shirt was positively indecent.

Nah. Don't tell him. Why spoil the fun?

''Anyway, she tearfully explained how she tried to take care of the kids after Muzzy's death.''

''Muzzy?''

Stephen shrugged. ''Go figure. The man was from Boston.''

''Muzzy from Boston.''

''Yeah.''

''Did he have family?''

''Nope.''

''And Lexi has only…''

''My mother, my brother and me.''

''Aha.''

''If you'd ever met Lexi, you'd know she wasn't the mothering kind.''

''I think I got the hint when she sent her kids to you via Speedy Delivery.''

He grimaced. ''I see what you mean. Don't get me wrong. Lexi's a sweet kid with a heart as big as the world. But she had a really rough childhood. She's blaming herself for being emotionally unprepared to care for quintuplets.''

''Mother Teresa would have been the only person I knew who would be emotionally prepared to care for quintuplets, and I even have my doubts she could have done it.''

''I know what you mean. In any event, Lexi has left the final decision for the children's future in my hands.'' He sighed, opening the door and waving at the little girls, who waved back from the seats in the Suburban. ''I'm meeting with a lawyer to discuss their options.''

''Options?'' Casey couldn't account for the way the mere word brought a lump to her throat.

''For their sake, I need to look at this situation from every angle possible.''

''Meaning?''

''Meaning a permanent home for them. Adoption. Either with me or a couple waiting for such an opportunity.''

''No one 'waits' for quintuplets.''

''True.''

The children were laughing and squealing now, and the noise carried easily to the clinic. Stephen waved again and Casey waggled her own fingers.

''You'd adopt them?''

''Sure. I knew from the first that Lexi sent them to me for that very reason. Despite her avowals to the contrary, I think she still hopes I'll keep them, but she's afraid to ask.''

''Do you want to keep them?''

He was quiet for several long moments, then said. ''I want what's best for them.''

''That's not what I'm asking. I'm asking if *you* want to keep them?''

He looked at her then, his eyes darkening with his concern for much more than the children alone.

"What do you think, Casey?"

She knew this was her chance to talk him out of the idea, but she couldn't. She wouldn't. So she pretended to misunderstand. "I think you've developed an affinity for Dr. Suess."

His smile was boyishly self-deprecating. "No. I'm asking what you would think if I *did* adopt them."

She shifted uncomfortably. "What I think is hardly relevant."

"I think it is."

Again, she purposely chose to take an impersonal approach. "As a psychologist, I see no reasons whatsoever why you shouldn't adopt them. Yes, you'd be bringing them into a single household, but I'm sure that condition will alter soon enough."

She cleared her throat when Stephen's gaze became even more penetrating. "What I mean is… you're young and quite good-looking.…"

He arched his brows.

"Which is to say that…blast it all, Pastor," she finally said in a rush. "Stop looking at me that way."

"What way?"

"Like you know something I don't."

"How could I know any such thing? I was merely asking your advice."

"And frankly, I think five little girls could do far worse than to be placed in the care of a man capable of being a loving and supportive father. Furthermore, by keeping them, you also open the door for Lexi to come to terms with her perceived shortcomings. Maybe she isn't ready to be an instant mother, but by seeing how the little girls flourish, she might discover she can be a doting aunt.''

"You still haven't answered my question.''

She shoved her hands into her pockets. "I think I've given you a very thorough analysis.''

"But I wanted a personal one.'' He cupped her face in his palms, the gesture so gentle that her toes curled inside her shoes.

"I don't think you're as blithely unaware of my interest in you as you pretend to be.''

"I—''

He stopped what she was about to say by pressing his thumb against her lips.

"Let me finish. I'm thirty-nine years old.''

Thirty-nine. He didn't look thirty-nine. Thirty-six, maybe. Thirty-seven at the most.

"I'm one of the only single ministers in this state—in the Midwest, for that matter. But my status as a bachelor has always been my choice. Some day, I knew I'd find a woman who would tempt me to alter that situation.''

Casey knew she should move, speak, anything to break the spell settling around her. For heaven's sake! This man was seriously considering adopting five little girls who were just beginning to explore "the terrible twos.'' In theory, it would be so easy to throw caution to the wind and say "Hell, yes, I'll be their mother.''

But Casey was thirty-five years old. Like Stephen,

she'd grown into her own emotional ruts and routines. She was used to having things her way, and the arrival of any child meant making enormous sacrifices in time and energy. It had taken Casey weeks to come to terms with the responsibilities of twins. But quintuplets *and* twins?

She couldn't even imagine the financial strain involved in feeding and clothing five kids the same age. Emotionally, she couldn't fathom the organizational skills so many children would involve. To add her own twins to that picture...

It boggled the mind.

Stephen stepped closer, his head bending. "I know we haven't known each other long enough for me to even presume..."

Go ahead. Presume.

"But I wanted you to know that I won't be thinking of the girls alone as I make my decision."

Then he kissed her, his lips so soft, so gentle, so reverent that a heat blazed through Casey's body—not just from the instantaneous desire that leapt into her blood. But because this man was so good to her, so good for her, so...

Perfect.

So why did their situation have to be so complicated?

Stephen drew back, smiling.

"I'd like to see you tonight."

"I—"

She couldn't think of a damned thing to say.

"I'll probably be late since I've got an appointment with a pediatrician and State Social Services. But if you're up to a late night, I'll meet you on the roof at nine. If not, I'll see you tomorrow.''

Say no. Don't get any deeper into this relationship.

But the only thing to leave her mouth was "I'll be there.''

"Good.''

He kissed her again, quickly, sweetly, leaving no doubt that he would stay longer if he could. Nor did he leave any doubt that once he had her alone on the roof he would kiss her again in a much more leisurely fashion.

"Until tonight,'' he said, then reluctantly released her and hurried to where the Suburban was beginning to rock from the antics of the impatient quintuplets.

Closing the door, Casey leaned her head against the cool panels, still bemused, aroused and confused.

A sudden sniff caused her to turn.

Erica stood in the hall, a tissue in her hand. Despite her wide grin, her eyes brimmed with tears.

"That's the most beautiful thing I've ever seen in my whole life,'' she said, laughing as she dabbed her lashes. "I always cry at weddings.''

"Weddings?'' Casey echoed weakly. "What are you talking about? The man didn't propose.''

"Not yet.''

"Erica—''

"No. Let me enjoy the moment,'' Erica said, holding up a hand. Then, turning back to the examination room, she offered, "The babies are due in September. I think an autumn ceremony would be beautiful.

Just remember, as your maid of honor, I look horrible in pastels.''

"WE ARE NOT GETTING married," Casey insisted later as she and Erica roamed through a pricey maternity boutique called Mama Bird. Despite Casey's warnings that Stephen would also be in Wichita, Erica had insisted that there was no other place to shop.

"My mother could cater."

"Get real, Erica. No one said anything about marriage."

"No one had to say anything."

"Erica," Casey cried. "Will you be reasonable and look at the facts? This isn't a case of marrying a man with a couple of kids, this is—*poof*—instant family."

"I know. Isn't it wonderful?"

"No. It's not."

Erica nudged her in the ribs. "Oh, lighten up. Lots of people have seven children in their families. Especially in the suburbs."

Casey rolled her eyes. "How many of them have seven children under the age of three?"

That point caused Erica's eyes to widen. "I guess you've got a point."

"Moreover, you've forgotten one very important fact."

"Which is?"

"*I* know that any sort of long-lasting relationship will involve seven children. *He* doesn't."

Erica's ebullient mood dimmed. "Damn. I forgot about that."

"No kidding. And while I've had a little time to grow used to the idea of taking care of twins, Stephen has had his own kids drop out of the blue."

"Via Speedy Delivery."

"Exactly."

"Do you think he'll balk at the idea of seven kids?"

Casey grimaced. "What do *you* think?"

Erica winced.

"Let's face it, Erica. Most men are *convinced* they want to be fathers by well-meaning wives. No man in his right mind would volunteer to go from bachelorhood to a family of eight."

"Nine. He'd have a wife to consider, too."

Nine. The number seemed even more awful to contemplate.

"Do you see now why I haven't told him?"

Erica nodded, then held a delicate pink shirt against Casey's chest. "Even so, I don't see that you have a choice. From my experience with twins, you have about two weeks before those babies will be impossible to hide. By the first of the month, you're going to look positively rotund. Midway through this pregnancy, you'll be as big as a house."

Casey scowled. "Thanks a lot."

"What are friends for, if not to be brutally honest?"

But Erica's grin was tinged with empathy, and unbidden, she drew Casey into her arms for a quick hug.

"Don't worry," she whispered. "These things have a way of working themselves out."

Casey nodded. But she couldn't see any way that this situation could end other than in separation.

STEPHEN GLANCED AT his watch, then continued to pace the sidewalk lined with expensive boutiques and jewelry shops. He'd already met with the lawyer, and after conferring with the woman over the choices available to him and the children, he'd been led to an inevitable decision.

He was going to be a father.

A sound that was half laugh, half snort escaped from his throat. In truth, the decision had been made the moment that he'd known Casey wasn't completely opposed to the idea. Already, he'd begun taking steps to clear up the paperwork. The children were with a child psychologist for the next hour, then he'd take them to the pediatrician, and make an appointment for the home study to be done.

He took a deep breath. From the moment that Casey had barreled into his life, so many things had happened to alter his way of living. He knew that he should feel some measure of panic. But he actually felt...

Joy. Sheer and utter joy.

When he caught the suspicious glance of a passerby, Stephen stopped and turned to the nearest window.

He knew it wouldn't be easy to be the father of quintuplets. But how could he send them away when they'd already wrapped their fingers around his heart? He was also fully aware that their presence would complicate other matters as well—life in Ruckerville, his relationship with Casey. But he would take each day as it came and trust in providence to provide a way. After all, Stephen knew with all his heart that coincidence hadn't brought any of them to this point.

He was in love.

For the first time in his life.

With Casey.

With his children. *His* children.

He blinked, focusing on the display in front of him—and as if an angel on his shoulder were prodding him on, the sun moved from behind a cloud. In an instant, the light caught a ring in the back of the case, causing the square-cut ruby with its flanking diamonds to shimmer.

No. He couldn't buy a ring. He was presuming far too much.

Wasn't he?

Stephen touched the glass with his hand, leaning closer, imagining the ring sliding onto Casey's delicate fingers. Everything about the setting seemed to symbolize his feelings for her—the fiery passion of the ruby, the constancy and strength of the diamonds.

Should he?

No.

Resolutely turning away, he took two steps, stopped, then turned and strode into the jewelry store.

Just as he'd told Casey, sometimes a person had to take a leap of faith.

Chapter Twelve

Casey returned home in time to briefly meet with Stephen, then exhausted, she was forced to excuse herself and go to bed.

Erica journeyed back to Manhattan the following day, leaving Casey with bags full of maternity wear, carpet and wallpaper samples for the nursery, and a glossy black-and-white photograph of her latest ultrasound.

To Casey, the black-and-white dots still resembled a Rorschach test, but with Erica's help, she'd been able to find evidence of two tiny heads and bodies. More and more, the twins were becoming real to her and not just a far-off dream.

Keeping her children foremost in her mind for the rest of the week, Casey tried her best to avoid coming into contact with Stephen—an easy-enough task since he'd been asked to serve as assistant Scoutmaster for the Cub Scout Jamboree. He was camping somewhere north of Ruckerville for most of the week.

To her delight—and infinite relief—Casey's contractor called during that time to inform her that his crew was still working on the front stoop, but the house was ready for paint and furnishings.

Hearing of her imminent move, the divorced mothers arranged a joint session with the unwed teenage mothers-to-be. They all talked and laughed and teased one another as they helped Casey paint and scrub and decorate. Then they loaded the few boxes of belongings Casey had brought with her and transferred them to the house.

Since Erica had promised to arrange for a moving company to send the rest of her furniture and belongings as soon as could be arranged, Casey saw no reason to delay moving into her new home. She spent an afternoon scavenging antique stores and thrift shops for pieces to augment her more spacious living quarters—an Edwardian dining room table, a gleaming brass bed and a walnut sideboard. But she hesitated in doing anything to the turret, which would soon become the nursery.

Since Stephen would probably insist on a tour of her new home, she couldn't let him see that she planned to paint the room off the master bedroom in pastel colors. She'd already chosen a pale sky blue for the ceiling and a teal green for the walls. With the help of some shelving, art paint and ready-made picket fencing, she planned to give the illusion that the turret was a country pasture. She'd ordered two pine cribs with bumper pads and quilts that were patterned with cartoon cows and chickens. Matching extra fabric would serve as a valance on the windows and cushions for the old rocking chair given to Casey by her grandmother.

It was only after her support groups had left her in the quiet of her new home, and Bert, Myrtle and Anne had dropped off a potted plant as a house-warming gift, that Casey realized she'd actually gone through with the whole venture.

She was a homeowner.

Her own home.

Not Stephen's.

The thought filled her with an inexpressible sadness, but the mood was tempered slightly when the phone rang for the first time.

"Hello?" she answered tentatively.

"Hi."

The moment Stephen's voice melted through the lines, her knees grew weak and she sank onto the carpeted floor.

"You're back," she said, commenting on the obvious.

"Yes. And imagine my surprise at discovering my assistant was no longer in residence."

She wrapped the phone cord around her finger. "Are you angry?"

"Why? Because you wanted some peace and quiet?" he teased. Then he offered more seriously, "No. I'm not angry. *Frustrated* might be a more apt description."

"Did you need me to do something for the church?"

"No. For me. I was hoping to get a welcome-home kiss."

"Oh," she breathed, feeling the air whoosh out of her lungs.

"But after a week with preadolescent boys, camp-fires and crude bathing facilities, you probably wouldn't have given me one, anyway."

"Oh, I don't know." She blushed at the uncon-scious intimacy of her tone.

"Why, Miss Fairchild…is that an invitation?"

"Maybe."

"Then I'll be over in fifteen minutes. See if you can't scrounge up something for us to eat. I'll bring the drinks."

The line went dead, but it took Casey a full minute before she realized that Stephen had taken her state-ment literally. The man was probably already on his way.

Running to her bedroom, she quickly showered and changed into her loosest jumper—one that would not accommodate her figure for much longer. Then she ran a comb through her hair, freshened her makeup and hurried to the kitchen.

Thankfully, the Ladies' Aid had also dropped by during the afternoon, and she had a salad, two cas-seroles, a cake and fresh bread to offer the pastor for dinner. Then, since the quintuplets would probably be accompanying him as well—after spending the week with Bert, Anne and Myrtle and their baby-sitter, Grace Smith, as their primary guardians—she grabbed a package of animal crackers to stave off their hunger until the lasagna could be properly heated.

At long last, breathless, her heart pounding, she sat on the bottom step in the foyer and waited for Stephen to arrive.

Tonight I'll tell him everything.

But hadn't she said the same thing a dozen times before?

Yes, but tonight there was no backing out. Stephen had to know the real reason for her arrival in Ruckerville. Somehow, she would think of a way to spill the news before he arrived.

But as the Suburban's motor roared into her driveway, she still didn't have a plan of action. The moment the doorbell pealed through the house, she smoothed her hair with her hands and jumped to her feet. After all, five little girls would not wait for her to decide how and when to inform Stephen of her pregnancy. Casey would simply have to rely on instinct.

As long as she told him.

She couldn't delay any longer.

Casey swung the door wide, her lips already spread in a welcoming grin.

But it wasn't the quintuplets who crowded her tiny stoop. It was a single man. Pastor Stephen Dubois.

He held a bottle of wine aloft. "I hope you don't mind, but I came without the entourage."

Casey wiped her palms down the folds of her jumper. Until that moment, she hadn't realized how much she'd counted on having the girls along to help "chaperone."

Or run interference.

"Am I still invited?" he asked, one dark brow lifting.

"Of course." Her laugh was more nervous than she had planned, but she held the door wide and accepted the gift of the wine. "How did you manage to find a baby-sitter? Didn't Grace need a break after being with them full-time?"

"Actually, I had volunteers."

"Who?"

"Your divorced mothers group decided to offer their skills. They were taking the unwed mothers-to-be and their own kids to the zoo this evening, so they volunteered to take the quints as well. Altogether, there are eleven women and seventeen children. By my calculations, the women were grossly understaffed, but they refused to take no for an answer."

Probably because they knew the pastor's destination and had matchmaking on the mind.

And then the door closed and Casey's mind went completely blank.

A warmth spilled into the narrow space at the bottom of the stairs, one that had nothing to do with the early-evening sunshine and everything to do with the tall, ruggedly built man who towered over her.

So lean.

So appealing.

So heart-wrenchingly impossible.

"I...uh...I made pasta. Well, actually, I warmed

up pasta. Nola Wilkens and the gang stopped by earlier.''

Stephen didn't speak. Instead, he moved toward her, his body crowding hers against the doorjamb. Then he was kissing her, his lips covering her own in a way that made his desire of her no secret.

Their mouths twined intimately, hands grasping for each other. Passion flared, jolting them like lightning with its intensity, and Casey couldn't think of anywhere she would rather be than in this house, in this man's arms.

When he finally drew back for breath, they were both trembling.

''I missed you,'' he murmured.

''You've been gone less than a week.''

''An eternity.''

''I don't think your Cub Scouts would agree with your estimation of the passage of time.''

''The parents who camped with us would.'' He cupped her cheeks, forcing her to look up at him. ''But, I don't care what they think.''

Then he was kissing her again, rocking her carefully erected defenses and leaving her clinging to him as if he were the only anchor in a whirling storm. But when his hands slid around her waist to draw her against him, she deftly sidestepped him, hurrying to the kitchen.

''I hope you like lasagna. If I'd had time, I would have whipped up a batch of my own famous tortellini. In college, I shared an apartment with three exchange students from Italy. They gave me a secret family recipe for a white sauce that will…''

Stephen's arms snapped around her waist and he hauled her back against his chest, his hands spreading wide.

''Why are you always running, Casey?'' The question was only half in jest. ''Don't you know what you do to me? Don't you know how much I want to—''

Casey knew the exact instant when the evidence Stephen cupped in his hands was absorbed by his brain. Closing her eyes, she wished with all her heart that things could be different. That her own babies wouldn't arrive so soon…or that the man she loved wasn't already the father of five.

But even as the thoughts raced through her head, she wondered how the situation could be changed. Not even for the love of Stephen Dubois would she wish away the children growing beneath her heart. Nor could she deny him the little girls who filled his days with joy.

Behind her, Stephen still hadn't moved, and she slipped from his arms, leaning against the counter a few feet away. For the first time, she made no attempt to hide her condition from him, and as she folded her arms beneath her breasts, the burgeoning of her stomach was unmistakable.

''You're…''

''Pregnant,'' she supplied softy when he couldn't seem to find the words to continue.

He glanced up at the ceiling as if drawing upon

the powers of heaven to help him. Then, raking his hands through his hair in a gesture of confusion that she'd come to adore, he sank into one of the chairs.

"You told me you weren't married—at least I assumed you weren't. I'm not sure if I ever really asked or—"

"I'm not married, Stephen. I've never been married."

He rested one of his forearms on the table and studied her with grave confusion. "The father…ran out on you, I suppose."

She shook her head. If only she could freeze this moment in time. Then she could think of the perfect way to allay his concerns and plead her own case.

Then again, she'd been searching for a way to express herself since arriving in Ruckerville.

"The father did not run out on me."

"Then you're still…" His hand waved in the air.

"No. The father was…an anonymous donor. I purchased the sperm after studying a catalog given to me by my doctor. Erica Beaman. Your cousin. The woman who arranged for me to come to Ruckerville."

He gazed at her for such a long time, she finally turned away and busied herself with wiping nonexistent spots from the silverware.

"I know that this will probably be impossible for you to understand—"

"I *have* heard of artificial insemination before, Casey."

"But have you heard about it from someone you were…dating?" she retorted quickly.

"Is that all we were doing? Dating?"

She couldn't look at him. Sinking into the chair opposite Stephen, she stared down at the fork and gaily patterned dishcloth in her hands.

"I don't know. I thought…I dared to hope…it was more."

She made the mistake of looking at him, then couldn't look away. His expression was so serious, so sad, so incredulous.

"I'm sorry, Stephen. I've tried to tell you a hundred times."

Again, the room filled with silence, and in those aching moments she knew again why Stephen had captured her heart. There were no recriminations, merely a bemused wonder.

"Why…"

She saw the word forming on his lips rather than heard it.

"Did I choose to become pregnant?" she finished.

He nodded.

"This year I turned thirty-five," she said, as if such a statement explained everything.

His brow rose in disbelief. "Don't tell me this was some reaction to a…midlife crisis. I won't believe you."

"No," she responded with utmost seriousness. "I did it in response to an emptiness. A need. An indescribable yearning to become a mother."

He offered a bark of laughter and rubbed his face

with his hands as if to ensure himself that the conversation was real and not a figment of his dreams.

"When did you—" he swallowed as his voice grew husky "—have the procedure done?"

She began to trace the pattern of the tablecloth with her thumb, knowing that she would have to tell this man more than she had ever told another living soul other than Erica. He deserved the whole truth.

"I think, before all the other details, you should know that this wasn't a whim on my part. I agonized over the thought of being a single mother long before I broached the subject with Erica."

She took a deep breath, plunging into the deep waters of her soul. "I was only nineteen when a cyst was found on one of my ovaries. In removing the cyst, half of the ovary was sacrificed, as well. Three years later, another cyst was found on the opposite ovary and I lost...all of it."

She cleared her throat and continued, refusing to lift her head for fear she would not continue.

"By the time I reached thirty, I was warned that subsequent scarring had not helped efforts. At that time, I was told that if I planned to have children, I should do so immediately."

Shrugging, she tried to add a note of levity. "In all that time, the only man I ever met who was worthy to share in the responsibility of bringing a life into this world was RJR-176—and even his cooperation ended after the donor stage."

She dared to peek at Stephen and found him watching her intently.

Jumping to her feet again, she paced the confines of the room. "In vitro was the most viable option for me, but even so, the procedure wasn't successful until the third try. I was given strict orders of bedrest the first trimester to avoid miscarrying. Then, when it became obvious that my life-style would only complicate an already difficult pregnancy, Erica arranged for me to come here."

Casey clutched her hands in front of her. "I never imagined that I would meet you. I never imagined that I would…grow to care for you so much."

His lips spread in a crooked, rueful smile. "Nor, I suppose, did you envision the arrival of quintuplets to complicate things even further."

"No," she admitted with a quick, irrepressible grin. "I can't say I ever foresaw such a complication—and I tried my best to imagine every contingency that might be thrown my way when a man…showed an interest in…"

"A relationship with you," he finished.

Relationship.

For so long, both she and Stephen had danced around proclaiming their feelings in words, but she knew in that instant how much Stephen had grown to care for her. With him, there would be no affair or short-lived liaison. A relationship to him meant a lifetime together.

Marriage.

"I'm sorry, Stephen," she whispered, her heart aching.

He stood, staring unfocused at a spot above his head. "No, you shouldn't feel sorry. A baby is..."

He didn't finish and Casey didn't bother to prompt him. She knew the stakes involved. This man had already begun proceedings to adopt five little girls—and the legalities couldn't be completed for another six months. To openly attach himself to a single, pregnant woman would be careless. To consider the added responsibility of Casey's own test-tube-generated offspring would be insane.

Especially since he wouldn't be contemplating one baby.

But two.

"Casey," he began slowly, glanced at her, then raked his fingers through the hair already tousled from similar gestures. "I've got to think this through. I..."

She waved away anything more he might have said. "I don't mind. Really. I know this has been a bit of a shock—and I know that you have more than yourself to consider right now."

His brows creased, and he suddenly seemed to become aware of the table, the plates, the bottle of wine she'd left on the counter.

"Suddenly, I'm not feeling very hungry."

Casey blinked at the tears that threatened to rise. "I don't think I could eat a thing, either. As a matter of fact," she said quickly, "I'm really beat after all the moving and everything." She paused only an instant before suggesting, "Maybe we should take a rain check on dinner."

It was obvious that he didn't want to leave. Just as it was obvious that he needed time to digest everything she'd told him.

"Really. I think we should call it a night, if you don't mind."

Worded that way, she left him no real option to stay. Even so, he asked, "You're sure?"

Suddenly weary, she nodded. "Yes."

He slid his fingers into the pockets of his jeans and studied her so completely, so intimately—his eyes still holding a gleam of desire.

Go, she silently prayed. *Go now before I beg you to stay.*

Just when Casey thought her resolve would snap, he nodded. "Okay. But I'm only going home to think, understand? Nothing between us has changed."

But both of their lives had been profoundly altered in the space of a few minutes, and Casey couldn't kid herself into thinking that anything could be as it had been before this night.

Turning, Stephen slowly walked into the foyer. Following him, knowing that she had to tell him the rest before he left, Casey called, "Stephen?"

His hand was on the knob, his body already disappearing through the slit of space made by the front door.

"Stephen, there's one more thing you have to know."

"Sure. What is it?"

Wringing her hands together, Casey held her breath, then dropped the bomb.

"Stephen, I'm not just having one baby. I'm having twins."

Chapter Thirteen

Casey had never seen anyone faint before—and certainly not anyone as strong and virile as Stephen Dubois. He hit the floor of the concrete porch with an audible crash, upending the wicker furniture left by the previous owner.

Panicked, Casey rushed to his side, rolling him onto his back. Already, there was a purplish bruise forming on his brow from where he'd connected with the concrete.

"Stephen?" she said, her heart thumping in her ears. "Stephen, wake up."

But he didn't respond, and filled with a fear like none she'd ever known before, she ran inside and called 911.

Seconds later, she heard the blaring whine of the siren attached to the nearby station. Generally, the horn sounded each Thursday evening at seven to announce a practice fire drill for the volunteer fire brigade, but this time, the emergency was real. Within five minutes, her street was crowded with firemen in bunker gear, a hook and ladder, ambulance, EMTs and dozens of curious neighbors.

Closing her eyes and moaning to herself, Casey realized that the whole community was probably aware that the pastor had fainted on her front doorstep. She'd already experienced the lightning-swift response of the grapevine on her own behalf, and knew for a fact that half the town owned a police scanner. Worse yet, after a whiff of smelling salts, Stephen was beginning to rouse, but the bump on his head had disoriented him so much that the only intelligible words he managed to utter were "Twins, twins, twins…"

Blushing furiously, Casey longed to close herself in the house and never show her face again. Within hours, Ruckerville would be buzzing—especially since she knew it was time to let the whole town know of her pregnancy. But when the EMTs assumed she would want to go with Stephen in the ambulance, she didn't have the heart to refuse. After all, it was her fault that he was in this sorry condition.

It was as they were all racing toward the hospital, siren wailing, tires screeching, that Stephen finally ceased his incoherent ramblings and opened his eyes.

Blinking away tears she hadn't even known had flooded her eyes, Casey grasped his hand.

"Wha…"

"You fainted," she said, instinctively interpreting his query.

He glanced from her to the eager EMTs.

"As near as we can gather, you hit your head on the concrete porch," one of them said.

His partner grinned. "As if the Scouts weren't enough for one week, now you're on your way to the hospital."

Stephen immediately grappled with the straps that held him down. "No, I'm fine...I..."

"Lie still, Stephen," Casey pleaded, spreading her hands wide over his chest. "Please. For me."

He instantly relaxed, and Casey caught the way the EMTs grinned and cast knowing glances at each other.

Stephen ignored them and grabbed her hand. "You aren't hurt, are you?"

She shook her head, then shifted uneasily, praying he wouldn't reveal her condition to the other men present.

Sensing her unease, Stephen relaxed and closed his eyes.

"Got a headache?" one of the men asked.

"A doozy," Stephen responded. But only Casey was aware that his fall wasn't entirely responsible for the pounding tension. He'd been so carefree and passionate when he'd arrived at her house for dinner. He'd left confused, discouraged...

And wounded.

Remembering that awful moment when she'd heard Stephen's head collide with the floor, Casey tried to pull her hand back, but Stephen wouldn't let go.

"Give me a couple of aspirin and stop the ambulance, guys. I'm fine. Really."

"I'm afraid you'll have to tell the doctor that. Judging by the bruise on your head, he'll be wanting some X rays."

"Dammit all to hell," Stephen muttered under his breath.

The two EMTs snorted in surprise at the unaccustomed curses coming from the local pastor, but Casey merely rolled her eyes. Once again, she'd given Stephen reason to swear.

STEPHEN WASN'T SURE at what point he blacked out again in the ambulance, but suddenly he opened his eyes and discovered that he was alone in a curtained cubicle of the hospital emergency room.

Wincing, he touched a hand to his brow, tenderly probing the golf-ball-size lump forming over his left eye. He'd never been a patient in a hospital before— never fainted.

Until today.

When Casey had told him she was pregnant with twins.

His eyes closed again and he forced himself to think.

Casey is pregnant.

Suddenly, everything made sense—her voracious appetite, the juvenile wallpaper books he'd glimpsed in her car, along with paint swatches in shades of pink, blue and yellow. And her clothes—shapeless, oversize dresses and drawstring pants.

Why hadn't he paid more attention to the changes occurring in her body? Why hadn't he been more observant of her bouts of nervousness when dealing with the quintuplets?

The curtain rustled, and he looked up to find Casey slipping into the narrow space next to the bed.

"You're awake," she said needlessly.

He nodded, then wished he hadn't moved at all when drums pounded in his head.

"They've taken X rays," she said, sliding her hands into her pockets. "There's no evidence of a fracture, just bruising. Maybe a slight concussion."

He made a face. "I feel like an idiot."

Her smile was slow and rueful. "I've never seen a man faint before—or a woman, either, for that matter. It's much less graceful in reality than it is in the movies."

"Thanks a lot."

Her hands balled into fists beneath the soft fabric of her dress and she shifted from foot to foot. "I'm sorry about what happened."

She looked so small, so uncertain....

So wonderful.

His voice was gruff and laden with weariness. "It's not your fault."

"I could have found a better way to break the news."

"I don't think that's possible, do you?"

Her laughter was soft, ironic, feathering over him with a silken caress. "I could have made you sit down first."

He grinned and she relaxed, her own smile widening.

Then, when the silence grew electric between them, she cleared her throat. "I guess I'd better leave you to rest some more. The doctor will be around to talk to you soon. In the meantime, the guys from the ambulance have volunteered to give me a ride home, so…" She stood where she was, her eyes hopeful yet sad. "I'll see you at work."

"Sure."

She was halfway through the curtain when he managed to clear his throat enough to say "Casey?"

"Yeah?"

He didn't think he'd ever tire of her sweet face, her innate appeal.

"I'll be in touch with you soon."

"Of course. After all, we have tons of correspondence that—"

"Not about business. We'll need to talk. About us."

She nodded, but he knew by her expression that she didn't dare hope anything could come from conversing with each other. After all, any decisions to be made had to include seven children.

Seven.

His head throbbed again.

"Bye, Stephen," Casey whispered. Then she was gone, and only the faint scent of her perfume remained to remind him of all he'd hoped this night might bring.

OVER THE NEXT FEW DAYS, Stephen tried his best to resolve the situation with Casey by reviewing every possible scenario in his head. Instinctively, he wanted to throw caution to the wind, propose and show her the ring he kept hidden in his desk drawer.

But as he became embroiled in the legalities of adopting the quintuplets, he soon discovered that matters would not be that easy. Although the children had been placed in his care by their stepmother and guardian, he would have to wait another six months before they became his own legal children. In that time, he could be visited at any time by the social worker assigned to his home study. Even as a minister, he had to prove to the world at large that he was financially, morally and emotionally responsible enough to care for the five girls.

So at a time when he wanted to rush ahead with his own plans for the future, he was forced to wait and pray that some sort of solution to the problem materialized out of thin air.

Unfortunately, such prudence caused an emotional rift to grow between them both. Within days, a pattern was set. Casey dropped by the rectory late in the afternoons—when she knew he would be busy tending to church business. She would read the list of jobs he'd left for her on her church calendar, then disappear in the cultural hall to work with her support groups. Except for a terse note that stated she'd decided not to attend the picnic, he didn't personally see or hear from her at all.

Sensing they both needed time to sort out their

feelings, Stephen didn't push for more contact with his assistant—even though he ached to see her. From Anne, he discovered that Casey had informed Nola Wilkens of her pregnancy—thereby ensuring that the rest of the town would know with record speed. From Bert, Stephen learned she'd begun to attend a La-maze class at the clinic. And from Myrtle, he'd dis-covered that Casey had begun making arrangements for her support groups to meet at her home.

Soon, the days faded into weeks, then months. Through it all, Stephen missed her—so powerfully, he'd wondered how he'd ever existed without her. But even now, with summer fading and autumn fast approaching, he didn't know how to end the impasse. None of the obstacles keeping him and Casey apart had altered. Nor had their circumstances. They were still two single adults struggling to provide for sev-eral children at once.

Pulling open the drawer to his desk, Stephen dug beneath a pile of envelopes and retrieved the velvet box that held the engagement ring he'd bought in Wichita. Leaning back in his office chair, he sat qui-etly in the darkness of his office, his thumb stroking the soft fabric.

Staring into nothingness, he tried to envision his life without Casey Fairchild, but he couldn't do it. Even now, with the emotional distance between them, he was comforted by the fact that she lived mere blocks away.

But how long would he be able to revel in such a luxury? How long before she grew tired of the Ruckerville grapevine, Founder's Day parades and side dishes of gravy?

Even as the thought popped into his brain, he dismissed it. Casey loved Ruckerville, and her enthusiasm about small-town life could not be denied. No, if anything were to chase her away, it would be the unresolved status of their relationship.

Dammit, why did life have to be so complicated? Stephen loved Casey. He wanted to marry her.

But was it fair to even ask? She had two babies on the way. Wasn't it the height of gall to demand she become the mother to five more, plus take on the rigorous duties also demanded of a pastor's wife?

But what was the alternative? A life alone? Losing the woman he loved? Or worse yet, terminating the adoption proceedings?

He couldn't do that. The girls needed him.

No.

His *daughters* needed him—and the quintuplets were his daughters as completely as if he'd helped give them life.

Even so, he wasn't blind to their needs. Already, thoughts of five sets of wardrobes, five sets of Barbie dolls, five sets of braces, five sets of prom dresses, were more than staggering.

To consider seven children under the age of three…the thought was unnerving—terrifying.

But letting Casey Fairchild walk out of his life was just as frightening.

Sighing, Stephen raked his hands through his hair,

wishing there was someone he could turn to for advice and...

Advice.

Snatching up the telephone, he punched the long-distance number and waited impatiently until a young boy answered, his voice cracking as he spoke.

"Hey, this is St. Paul's. What do you want?"

Stephen blinked, surprised by the blunt query. Then he realized his brother Jean-Luc must have commandeered his youth group into manning the phones.

"May I speak with Father Jean-Luc, please?"

"Who is this?"

The response was phrased as a challenge, but Stephen supposed the boy was doing his best to follow telephone etiquette.

"Tell him it's Pastor Etienne Dubois," Stephen said, employing the French version of his name for Jean-Luc who spent most of his teenage years in Paris with their father. A pause ensued, and Stephen clarified, "His brother."

"Are you one of those friar dudes?"

"No," Stephen said patiently. "Father Jean-Luc and I were raised by the same parents."

"Like...in foster care?"

"No. We shared the same *biological* parents. We're siblings."

"You gotta be kidding! I didn't think priests could do that stuff."

Stephen grinned, since the boy was assuming Jean-Luc's vows of celibacy were somehow retroactive.

"When I knew him, Father Jean-Luc wasn't a priest," he said, trying a new tack.

"So who are you again?"

"Pastor Etienne—"

"Pastor. What the hell's a pastor?"

"We're the priests who can date."

"Get outta here!" the boy exclaimed. "You mean you and a woman can—"

"Hello, this is Father Jean-Luc. May I help you?"

Stephen chuckled softly, a warmth flooding his chest at the familiar tones and inflections. "That depends. Do *you* know the difference between a priest, a brother and a pastor?"

Muffled noise conveyed to Stephen that Jean-Luc had covered the phone with his hand. Stephen could almost see Jean-Luc shooing the youngsters out of his office, slamming the door, then sprawling into the rickety chair behind his desk.

"To what do I owe the pleasure of this call, Etienne? I haven't heard from you in what…six months? Seven?"

"Sorry about that."

"And all those newsy letters," Jean-Luc continued. "It's a wonder that I've kept up with them all."

"I've been busy."

"So I hear. Congratulations…Papa."

Stephen grimaced. "Mom was on the phone as soon as she heard the news about the proposed adoption from me, I take it."

"The woman should own stock in AT&T."

Stephen could hear the squeak of the chair and was

sure that Jean-Luc had plopped his feet on the blotter of his desk.

"How are the little rug rats?" his brother inquired lazily.

"Energetic."

"Fun?"

"Undoubtedly."

"Scary?"

"Absolutely."

In one brief exchange, the tension in Stephen's shoulders began to ease. If he closed his eyes, he and Jean-Luc could be sharing their grandmother's attic bedroom during the annual Christmas Eve reunion and exchanging the verbal shorthand they'd developed as kids.

"I envy you, you know," Jean-Luc said, and there was no disguising the wistfulness in his tone. "But I think a priest with five daughters would raise a few eyebrows."

"Trust me, I've raised a few brows of my own here in Kansas."

"I hope no one's giving you grief about taking in family."

"No. It's a bit of an unusual circumstance, but most of my congregation applauds me for doing my Christian duty."

There was a beat of silence, then Jean-Luc asked, "So what's wrong?"

"I, uh..." Stephen stalled, wondering how to approach the subject of Casey with a man who would never marry.

"Ahh. It must be the woman, then."

Stephen grew very still. He'd said nothing about Casey to his mother, so either Jean-Luc had experienced a vision, or someone else had been telling tales.

"I heard from Erica Beaman," Jean-Luc confirmed. "She sought me out for some advice. It seems that she sent one of her patients to Ruckerville. The woman was expecting twins, and Erica thought the country life would do her good. Instead, the patient—who had taken a job as the assistant to the pastor—has fallen in love with her boss."

Stephen's hand curled into a fist around the ring box he'd begun to hold for "luck" any time he worked alone. He'd sensed Casey loved him—he'd *known* she loved him. But to have the declaration come to him third-hand merely underscored the desperateness of the situation.

"And now *I* come to you for advice," Stephen said slowly. "How ironic."

"That's what family is for," Jean-Luc said, his voice low and thoughtful and filled with concern. "Unfortunately, I don't have a clue of what to say to help you sort through the tangle. Five kids all at once is a shock to any married man, let alone a single pastor. Add a romance to that, a woman who is already pregnant, and a pregnancy that will result in another two babies... Frankly, even the *National Exposure* wouldn't touch the situation with a ten-foot pole."

"So what do I do?"

"The right thing."

"What is the right thing?"

Jean-Luc took a deep breath. "I don't know. I could offer the same logic I'd give anyone else coming to me for counseling—pray, study, listen to your heart. But I know you've done that all along. The only other words of wisdom I could suggest is that you make sure, whatever you do, that you can live with the choice you've made—happily, without reservation—no matter what anyone else might say. If you can do that, the decision you've made is the right one."

Stephen's fingers uncurled, and he stared down at the ring in his hand. "No regrets, huh?"

"You don't want to look back on this moment fifty years from now and say, 'I wish...'"

"But what if my decision doesn't correspond with the lady's? What if I decide to take a chance, but she can't bring herself to do the same?"

"It's a risk you'll have to take. But judging by what Erica has told me about Casey Fairchild, I wouldn't sell the woman short."

"You haven't even met her."

"No, but I'm well acquainted with you. If she's got you tied in knots like this, I know I'm going to love her."

Stephen offered a choked laugh. "Why not? I do."

"So take a leap of faith."

Stephen stiffened as his brother offered the same words that had filled Stephen's head when he'd bought the ring. Brushing his thumb over the dome-shaped box that held the symbol of his love for Casey, Stephen knew there was only one possible course of action—no matter how crazy it might be.

He and Casey belonged together.

And it was up to him to see that he could convince her of the same thing.

Chapter Fourteen

Four months, Casey thought with a sigh. She'd been in Ruckerville more than four months now. And for three of those, she'd seen Stephen less than a handful of times.

Sighing, Casey surrendered to the fatigue she'd been battling all day—all week—and collapsed in the rocking chair. Around her, the nursery was nearly transformed. With the help of the friends she'd made in town—as well as the ever-faithful Bert, Myrtle and Anne, who visited her once each day—the walls and ceiling had been painted as she'd originally planned. The hardwood floors had been refinished and polished to perfection.

Smiling, Casey had to admit that her farmland motif was far more wonderful than she ever would have imagined—but not through her own efforts. She'd soon discovered that Bert was a master woodworker. Not only had he applied the picket fencing, but he'd added molding and hand-carved shelving to resemble telephone poles, animals and a distant barn. An old thrift-shop dresser had been transformed into a tractor, and the changing table, a wagon.

Anne had proved to be a master seamstress. She'd made valances over each window in the shape of puffy white clouds, then had hung sheer net curtains, employing the age-old technique of net darning to give the impression of raindrops dancing over the fabric.

And Myrtle...

Myrtle had amazed them all. After taking the measurements of the floor, she'd hooked a massive rug "to keep the babies from catching a chill from the floor." The pale greens and sages of the two-dimensional grass was interspersed with embroidered wildflowers and wandering vines.

In addition to all the furnishings, there were stuffed animals given to her by members of her support groups, hand-edged receiving blankets, knitted booties, quilts, frilly dresses, tiny college jerseys and two incredible crocheted baby shawls fashioned by Nola Wilkens herself.

The room was perfect.

Well, nearly perfect.

All that needed to be changed was Casey's spirits.

Sighing, Casey leaned her head against the back of the rocker and pushed her feet against the floor, hoping to ease the ache in her back and the weariness in her bones.

She knew she should be ecstatic. Less than four weeks remained before her due date. She had a beautiful home, a job with flexible hours, a bright future ahead of her, and a physician who'd taken a six-week vacation in order to tend to her needs. Who was she to complain?

Opening her eyes, she lifted the edge of the curtain, wincing at a sharp twinge of pain that shot through her back. Ignoring the Braxton-Hicks contractions that had plagued her all morning, she leaned forward. Not enough to draw attention, but enough to allow her to see the end of the street.

Since the quintuplets had begun going to "structured play" at the local civic center at noon each weekday, Casey had begun to watch for Stephen's car, hoping to catch a glimpse of the pastor as he zoomed by. Then, two hours later, she watched again.

The infrequent spottings were torture. Due to her awkwardness and lack of mobility, she'd given up going to the rectory. Instead, she held her support groups in her own home. In addition to those originally formed, she'd added one for parents of handicapped children, and another for teenagers. The extra meetings had gradually consumed the hours allotted to her in her part-time status, and Stephen had fallen back on volunteers and the Ladies' Aid Society to help with clerical work.

Casey regretted the emotional and physical distance that had formed between them, but she knew there was no other way. All she needed to verify she was doing the right thing was to catch a glimpse of Stephen's face when he saw her stomach. Because of their infrequent meetings, he was rarely prepared for how much she'd changed from the previous encounter. The invariable expressions of wonder, horror and fear were enough to convince her that he wasn't in a position to speak to her coherently, let alone discuss anything of a personal nature.

Too bad.

For the first time in her life, she found herself longing for the sympathetic ear of a spiritual mentor.

"None of that," a voice demanded from the doorway.

Casey glanced up to find Erica frowning at her. She extended one of the warm mugs of cocoa she held in Casey's direction.

"Did you turn up the heat?" Casey asked.

"Yes, ma'am."

Casey didn't argue when Erica snagged an afghan from the "wagon" and spread it over her legs and enormous tummy.

"I bet we get a storm," Casey said, pretending that she'd been looking at the weather from her vantage point at the window. She massaged her back when the ache deepened to a dull throb. She still had a month until her due date, but her back was already killing her and her face and hands were swollen beyond belief.

"A full moon, too," Erica commented, sinking onto the second rocking chair, one provided by the Cub Scouts as a service project. Casey hadn't had the heart to tell them that—other than occasional visitors—there would be no need for another chair.

Sighing in delight, Erica nudged the glider into

motion and took a sip of her cocoa. "This is good stuff," she remarked after a single taste.

"It's one of Anne's concoctions."

"The woman is a wonder. I don't think I've ever had better-smelling laundry in my life."

Casey blinked back the ever-present tears. Anne had given her an empty mayonnaise jar filled with her herbal waters for Casey's own wash, then another pretty cut-glass jar that held a different rinse for the babies' things.

"I didn't say a thing that should make you cry," Erica remarked.

"I know." Casey sniffed. "I can't help it." Searching in the pockets of her largest maternity house robe, she located a handkerchief and dabbed her eyes. "Bert and Myrtle and Anne are ready to move into their new apartment, and they want me to come see it as soon as I can. Stephen has even hooked an elevator-type contraption to the stairs so I don't have to climb them."

The thought made her sob.

"I don't think the elevator was installed for your benefit."

"I know," Casey sobbed. "It's just that he thinks of everything." She began to cry in earnest. "So why can't he think of a way for us to be together?"

Erica set her mug on the changing table and hurried to comfort Casey.

"I'm sorry," Casey cried out. "I don't know why I get so emotional."

"I think pregnancy, quintuplets, support groups

and being in love might have something to do with
it all."

"But I don't want to be this way. I want to be…"

"What?" Erica asked gently. "What do you want
to be?"

Casey's chin trembled. "I want to be happy. I
want everything to be perfect."

Eric sighed, brushing the hair from her face. "But
Casey, life is never perfect. If it were, we'd be bored.
And like you've said a hundred times, what would
you do to change the situation? Without your twins,
you never would have met Stephen. Without Stephen, the quintuplets might never have had a stable
home and you would have never believed yourself
capable of mothering more than one child at a time.
The quints gave him love and adoration, but they
gave you confidence in yourself."

Casey began to cry again, clutching at Erica as if
she were a lifeline. "What am I going to do? What
am I going to do?"

She cried for some time, long, heartrending sobs
that seemed to rip through her body and leave her
physically aching. She cried for all the wonderful
things that had come into her life, and all the wonderful things that seemed destined to remain out of
reach. She cried at finally falling in love, at becoming
a mother, at finding a place that felt like home.

Erica did her best to soothe Casey. She held her
close, rubbed her back and rocked her to and fro as
if Casey were no more than a youngster herself. And

through it all, she kept saying, "It will be all right. It will be all right."

But how could anything be truly "right" ever again?

At one point, the doorbell rang and Erica gently disengaged herself. Leaning back in the chair, her eyes closed, Casey tried her best to control her emotions, but the tears wouldn't stop. The sorrow locked in her chest and gripped her muscles, making her head pound and her eyes ache.

Distantly, she heard Erica's murmured conversation from the front of the house. Whipping a tissue from a box next to her chair, Casey attempted to dry her eyes, wincing at another twinge of pain. The weather made it difficult for her to tell how much time had passed, but she supposed that Bert, Anne and Myrtle had dropped by for their daily visit.

But when she heard footsteps in the hall, there was only a single pair. Covering her eyes with her hands, Casey offered a hiccoughing sob as Erica returned.

"Did you send them away?"

"No. She let me in."

The low tones were masculine and rich, and her hands dropped to her lap. Then, finding Stephen standing in the doorway, she began to cry again and quickly hid her face.

"Go away. I don't want you seeing me like this," she wailed.

"Like what?"

"Like…like…"

She shuddered when his arms wrapped around her

shoulders and she was drawn against the solid wall of his chest. Somehow, she turned her head, fitting perfectly into the hollow of his shoulder. Then she was grasping huge handfuls of his sweatshirt as if she feared he might take her advice and leave.

"You look beautiful," he whispered against her ear, before brushing a kiss against her hair. The caress was as soft as a butterfly's, but oh, so electrifying.

"Don't lie to me, Pastor Dubois. I've already corrupted you enough."

"How so?"

"I've tarnished your reputation—"

"Hardly."

"Upset your schedule—"

"Impossible."

"Ruined your life."

"Never."

Tipping back, she looked at him through the wavering sight caused by her tears. "I made you curse in public. Several times."

His smile was gentle as his broad, strong hands wiped the tear tracks from her cheeks. "I don't remember having a gun to my head."

"No, but I made you lose your control."

"Mmm." His expression was smug. Tender. And too achingly real for her to bear. "On that count, I will agree. You made me lose my control over and over again. But not from anger. Never from anger."

He kissed her then, his lips brushing hers with infinite gentleness. But what had begun as a sweet caress grew more and more sure, undeniably hungry, until his head tipped and her mouth opened to invite the caress of his tongue.

Clinging to him, she prayed that this moment would never end. She didn't know what had inspired him to come to her or how long he would stay. But for now, he was hers and he loved her.

Stephen broke free, hugging her tightly against him, kissing her cheek, her jaw.

"I love you."

For a moment, Casey thought the words were a product of her brain, but when Stephen repeated them, his lips brushing against the delicate skin of her ear, she knew he'd spoken them aloud.

"Wha—"

She tried to back away, to read his expression, gauge his mood, but he held her tightly.

"Shh. Just listen, okay? I've rehearsed this moment a dozen times, and I want to say everything I've planned before you interrupt me. Please."

She nodded, squeezing her eyes closed and clutching at him, breathing deeply of his scent, knowing that he had come to say goodbye.

He took a deep breath, and she felt the way it shuddered through his body as he began. "I've been doing a lot of soul-searching. I don't ever remember spending so much time on my knees on my own behalf, but with so much riding on this single moment, I knew I couldn't afford to make a mistake. Not with so many lives hanging in the balance."

Casey bit her lip, praying that she could survive the blow.

"I know there will be those who will think I've—*we've*—gone off the deep end for even considering...what I'm considering...or rather would like *you* to consider..."

He took another deep breath. "Hell, I thought I'd rehearsed this enough, but evidently not."

Casey squeezed her eyes even more tightly closed. "What? Tell me, Stephen. Tell me what you want to say."

Tell me quick while I still have strength to bear it.

"I think we should get married."

The words were so different from what Casey had expected to hear that she waited for some sort of catch. But when Stephen remained silent and grew as still and tense as she, she wriggled backward enough to study his features.

His jaw was tense, and lines of weariness bracketed his mouth. But he wasn't teasing. He was dead earnest. And...hopeful.

"What?" she breathed.

"I think we should get married."

She opened her mouth, but he placed a finger on her lips and allowed a few inches of space between them.

"I know what you're thinking. The idea is nuts. By combining our families, we'll have seven mouths to feed. But so what? There are families all over this state—this country, this world—with more children than that."

He held up a hand to forestall any argument she might have made, but Casey was so stunned, she couldn't have uttered a word.

"Look, I know I'm no bargain."

"No, Stephen, I—"

Again, he placed a finger on her lips.

"I've looked at the whole situation realistically for some time. I make a pastor's salary. My job has lousy hours, constant interruptions and incredible demands on my time. As my wife, you'd be subject to the same crazy life-style. But I also know that we'd have a good life together. We might have to employ some creative budgeting, but there would always be food on the table and love to spare. And I know we could be happy. All of us. Together. As a family."

The tears sprang into her eyes again, but this time, they were tears of joy. Stephen's passionate appeal had resonated with his love for her, with his need for her. And until she'd stumbled into his life, Casey had never really felt needed before. Not like this. Not in a way that made her body feel alive and young and filled with energy.

"Yes," she whispered.

But Stephen didn't seem to hear. "I know I've been avoiding you these past months—but please don't think it was because of you or your..." He nodded in the direction of her stomach. "It didn't have anything to do with that—I mean, other than to make me take a step back and really analyze the situation."

"Yes, Stephen," she said again.

"And if you want proof that I meant to ask you long ago, I've got it. Here. In my pocket."

He tunneled his fingers into the pocket of his jeans and withdrew a velvet ring box. Before Casey had a chance to catch her breath, he flipped the lid to reveal a beautiful ruby-and-diamond engagement ring.

"I bought it when I went to Wichita to meet with the lawyer about adopting the girls. The moment I saw it, I knew I wanted you to become my bride. But then I got mired in all the legalities of the adoption, and you had your twins to worry about."

He took the ring from the box, tossing the container onto the floor.

"But I want you to wear it. I love you, Casey. I can't live without you. I can't wait for your own children to be born so that we can all be together—the way it's meant to be."

He broke off and she blinked, a tear coursing its way down her cheek.

"Damn," he muttered. "I've bungled again and made you cry and—"

She shook her head. When he would have snatched the ring away, she caught his hand.

"I'm just waiting for you to shut up so you can put it on my finger," she said tremulously.

Stephen's eyes flared with sudden elation.

"You mean it? You'll marry me?"

She smoothed a hand over her stomach. "We'll all marry you," she said coyly.

Stephen laughed in triumph, but he was shaking as he guided the ring toward her finger.

"As touching as this scene has been," a voice said from the doorway, "I don't think it's a good idea to put the ring on just yet."

They both started, staring at Erica. Distantly, Casey wondered how long her friend had been standing there—then prayed she meant to leave again as soon as possible.

"Why not?" Stephen asked, his tone clearly challenging Erica's insistence that Casey's finger remain bare.

"Because, as a doctor, I think it's my duty to point out that Casey's hands have swollen to twice their size." She was fumbling with the gold chain looped around her neck. "And since the hospital frowns on its patients wearing jewelry—rings, especially—after admission, you may as well leave it off." Her eyes twinkled. "But I think we can bend the rules a little and let you wear it around your neck."

When both Casey and Stephen stared at her blankly, she huffed in mock irritation and held out the chain. "Evidently, neither one of you has noticed that Casey's water has broken. So in my opinion, it's time to go. I've already called the ambulance. Stephen, will you be riding with us or following in your own car?"

"An ambulance?" Stephen breathed. "Is something wrong?"

"Merely a precaution," Erica said with a smile. "I'd like to monitor the babies for any distress. Twins can sometimes have problems."

From that moment, Casey's world exploded into

chaos. Images and sensations crowded one on top of the other—the dampness of her skirt, the engagement ring being threaded onto the chain and the cool chain slung around her neck. Then there were bags to find as a siren wailed, and burly EMTs helped Casey settle onto a stretcher.

Just when she thought she'd caught her breath—pain ripped through her body. Clinging to Stephen's hand, she cried out, feeling the cool wind brush her cheeks as she was wheeled to the waiting vehicle.

"Good luck, Casey!" she heard one of her neighbors call. Then the rear doors slammed shut and she was crowded against an EMT, Erica and Stephen.

"Drugs," she gasped when another pain shot through her back.

Erica grinned.

Stephen turned pale.

"That's my girl. I wondered when you would admit to yourself, let alone me, that you've been suffering from more than Braxton-Hicks spasms all afternoon."

Casey groaned. "You could have warned me."

"Why spoil all the fun? Besides, the cards were stacked against you. Storm, full moon, bad mood, marriage proposal. The babies were bound to come tonight."

The ambulance made a sharp turn and Casey pulled at Stephen's hand—only loosening her grip when she noted the tips of his fingers were growing purple from poor circulation.

"I didn't agree to marry you in the throes of labor.

I'm not out of my head. Not yet. I haven't had any drugs. I said yes of my own free will."

Stephen's eyes widened, and he glanced at Erica in concern.

Erica snickered. "She's referring to transition. Women in labor can sometimes become...extreme during the last stage of labor. Either they scream at their husbands or start seeing little green men on the ceiling. But she's sane. Trust me."

"You're sure?"

"Absolutely. She's going to be fine, I promise." Erica's grin became even more mischievous. "But since you've popped the question, you've just been promoted to Lamaze coach until we reach the hospital. Go ahead, Papa. Now's the time to start bonding with your babies."

Stephen's skin turned from gray to green. "What do I do?"

"Breathe," Erica stated in a wicked drawl. "Both of you."

THE TWENTY-MINUTE DRIVE to the Regional Medical Center seemed like an eternity to Stephen. Following Erica's lead, he'd tried his best to keep Casey calm and focused on the task at hand, while at the same time he felt completely powerless and unsure of himself.

But as Casey was rushed down the hallway of the maternity suite for the planned cesarean section and he was left to wait outside the double doors, Stephen became aware of the true meaning of helplessness.

He loved this woman. Heart and soul. What would he do if something happened to her? He'd already lived through hell in the last few months. How much more awful would it be if he'd been allowed a glimpse of heaven, only to be thrown into torment again?

Needing some outlet for his fear, he began to pace. Twelve steps to the window of the waiting area, turn, thirty steps to the elevator banks, turn.

Soon, he drew the attention of the floor nurse. She offered him a bland smile. Evidently, she was used to women being rushed into the delivery room and men wandering the corridors in panic.

"Good evening, Pastor."

He nodded a greeting as he passed, took twelve steps, turned.

"It's sweet of you to accompany one of your parishioners in the ambulance."

"She's not one of my parishioners. Well, she is, but not really."

The woman's brows rose quizzically. She waited until he'd made his way to the elevators, turned and come back before saying "Oh?"

"That's my fiancée."

The nurse's jaw visibly dropped—and at any other time, Stephen supposed he would have laughed at her shocked expression. After all, the woman had seen him clinging to Casey's hand and had been forewarned by the ambulance that a pair of twins were about to be delivered.

"Your...fiancée?" she breathed.

He opened his mouth to explain, but the circumstances were far too complicated and involved. And since his pacing was the only thing keeping him from rushing to press his face against the window of the swinging double doors, he increased his speed.

"Pastor Dubois!"

He jumped, whirling, hoping that Erica had appeared to report Casey's progress. But it was Anne who marched down the hall, Myrtle rushing to keep up, and Bert bringing up the rear. Between the three of them, they managed to hold on to five toddlers dressed in denim overalls and ruffled, print T-shirts.

"How is she?" Bert huffed.

"She's been taken in there," he said, jerking a thumb at the suite of delivery rooms.

"What?" Myrtle shouted.

"Baby!" Anne bellowed in her ear. "Casey's having her twins!"

"Fins? Why'd she want us to bring fins to the hospital? Shouldn't she be having those kids of hers instead of lollygagging around in the therapy pool?"

Anne rolled her eyes.

"We came as soon as we heard Casey had been brought here by ambulance," she said, raising her voice when the toddlers begged to be let loose, then ran to the waiting room to play hide-and-seek amid the furniture. "Nola Wilkens heard it on her police scanner."

Stephen hadn't thought the day could hold any more surprises, but he'd evidently been wrong.

"Nola Wilkens has a scanner?"

"Yes, I do, Pastor," Nola said as the elevator doors swung wide and she strode into the corridor. "I've already started a phone tree to notify everyone who should know—her support groups, her neighbors, her..."

"Hey!"

A stunned silence cracked the bedlamlike noise, which had begun to invade the maternity ward as another elevator opened to disgorge a half-dozen people who had raced to the hospital from Ruckerville.

They all whirled at once to regard the nurse who had stood up and was now glaring at them.

"This is a hospital, not a gymnasium!" she snapped. "You will all be quiet, or I'll have security escort you from the premises." Her lips pursed. "In fact, there shouldn't be anyone here but family."

She pointed a finger at Stephen. "You say you're the woman's fiancé?"

Her disbelief was patent, but Stephen nodded. Unfortunately, his response caused those who gathered around him to erupt into cries of delight and congratulations.

"Stop, *stop, stop!*" the nurse bellowed.

Still staring frostily in Stephen's direction, she pointed to the quintuplets, who had discovered a box of toys kept in a trunk near the wall.

"Whom do they belong to?" she demanded.

"I'm their father," Stephen announced proudly.

The nurse scowled. "Do you mean to tell me that

woman gave birth to five children at once and you still had the *nerve* to get her pregnant again?''

Stephen shook his head. ''No. The quints aren't her biological children, but Casey is already like a mother to them.''

Clearly, the nurse was confused. ''I see. So the twins on the way are...''

''Mine,'' Stephen admitted.

''And your church lets you do that?'' she gasped in horror.

''They aren't my biological children. I only met their mother last spring.''

''And you still plan to...'' The words dangled in the eerie silence.

''Marry her?'' Stephen supplied. ''Yes. As soon as possible.''

The double doors from the delivery suite whooshed open and a petite woman dressed in surgical scrubs emerged. ''I'm supposed to usher father Dubois to the nursery.''

''I'm not a father, I'm a pa—'' Stephen flushed, realizing the woman meant to employ the term *father* in a completely secular way.

''This way.''

The woman gestured for him to follow as she held the door wide.

Stephen rushed forward. ''Is she all right? Casey. The mother. Is she...''

''She's a little busy right now, but she asked me to introduce you to someone,'' the woman said, her eyes twinkling. ''I was told by Dr. Beaman to settle your nerves. Most folks call me Nurse Molly, and I'm a pro with new fathers, so I promise you're in good hands.''

She stopped in front of a bank of windows shrouded with blinds. ''Stand right here. You'll be able to see best from this spot.''

''The baby,'' Anne whispered. ''The baby must be in there.''

Before the mechanized doors could shut, the waiting crowd flowed past the checkpoint and toward the nursery.

''Hey! You can't do that! Only family can go in there!'' the floor nurse cried.

''We are family, ma'am,'' Bert said as he helped Myrtle shuffle forward.

''Homely?'' Myrtle bellowed. ''Sure, she's homely, Bert. But no one said nurses had to be pretty, now, did they?''

The nurse's cheeks flushed, and she shook a fist in the air, demanding that order be restored. But Nola Wilkens merely patted her on the back and proudly said, ''That's our pastor. He's getting married, you know.''

The nurse lifted her hands in defeat just as the blinds covering the nursery window rattled, then lifted.

Within seconds, Nurse Molly appeared, wheeling a plastic incubator in front of her. Stopping beneath the windows, she pulled aside the light covering of blankets to reveal the tiniest, sweetest baby Stephen had ever seen in his life. The little body could have fit in the palm of Stephen's hand, but its eyes were wide and curious, its hand waving in the air as if to greet the hushed audience.

"It's a boy," Nurse Molly announced over the intercom. "Four pounds, one ounce, sixteen inches." She bent to retrieve supplies from the bottom shelf of the cart. Then she began to dress the baby in a teeny-tiny diaper, a blue knit cap and an undershirt emblazoned with the hospital's logo. Finally, after she was sure that the baby was properly dressed, she tightly wrapped him in his blankets again.

Just as she finished, another scrub-garbed woman burst into the nursery.

Pressing his hands to the window, Stephen fought to catch a glimpse of what must be the second twin. The wait was interminable as the nurse cleaned and charted and handled the infant. But at long last, she placed the bundle into another plastic incubator.

There was a brief silent exchange between the two nurses. The intercom clicked again.

"Another boy, four pounds even, fifteen and three-quarter inches," Nurse Molly said as her co-worker disappeared again.

Repeating the same ritual she'd followed with the first baby, Nurse Molly dressed his brother.

Not able to wait any longer, Stephen tapped on the window.

"They're so little," he said.

Although he doubted Nurse Molly could hear him through the glass, she must have read his lips because she moved to the intercom and gestured to the phone receiver on Stephen's side of the glass.

To his surprise, by lifting the phone, only he was able to hear the nurse as she explained, "Multiples are usually premature, which accounts for the low birth weight. But the boys are both healthy and strong—"

She was cut off when the second baby began to scream in outrage at the indignity of being stared at by so many people.

"How's Casey?" Stephen asked, plugging his free ear with a finger as the wail from the baby seeped over the phone and the ooh's and aah's from the people surrounding him threatened to drown out coherent thought.

"She's uh…"

His heart stopped, then lurched to painful life again at Nurse Molly's hesitation.

"What's wrong?" he demanded, suddenly cold.

"Nothing's wrong, but…"

Someone must have called to her, because she held up a finger to show she'd only be gone a minute. Stephen waited, dread thick on his tongue as Nurse Molly disappeared into the back room.

Oblivious to the mirth and jokes being bandied about by the folks from Ruckerville, he forced himself to remain calm. He took quick breaths, sucking air into his lungs to keep the wooziness at bay as he tried not to imagine what was happening in the delivery room. Through it all, a silent litany of prayers raced through his head.

Please, please, dear Lord. Keep her safe. Keep her safe.

Then Nurse Molly was darting back into the nursery. But with her back turned, Stephen couldn't tell what had required her complete attention. Briefly, he realized that his weren't the only babies being born on this day, in this hospital. Even so, he wished that Nurse Molly would finish with her task and allay his fears.

He was about to rap on the window again, when the woman turned, revealing that she had been caring for another baby. Gently, she placed the bundle in an incubator, secured a pink cap on its head, then wheeled the baby to the window.

Stephen briefly looked away, searching the sea of faces for the other new father, but he couldn't see a thing. In the scant minutes that had elapsed, at least a dozen more visitors had arrived from Ruckerville.

A tap on the window caused Stephen to start, and seeing that Nurse Molly was ready to speak again, he lifted the receiver to his ear, his movements wooden and automatic.

"A girl. Three pounds, nine ounces, fifteen and a half inches," she announced.

"Whose?" Stephen croaked.

The woman's lips twitched. "Yours," she said, clearly enjoying herself. "Ms. Fairchild wasn't carrying twins. She was carrying triplets."

Stephen felt the receiver drop from his lax fingers. His mouth opened, and he desperately tried to speak.

Triplets…triplets…triplets…

Everything around him tilted and jumped.

Eight children. *Eight!* he thought in amazement. *And I'm the father of them all.*

Then his knees buckled and the floor rushed up to meet him.

"HE FAINTED?" CASEY asked in amazement as Erica opened the curtains to her hospital room and allowed the late-morning sunshine to stream inside.

"Yep."

"He'll never forgive me. That's the second time I've made him faint."

Erica grinned. "I should have warned the nurses and made sure he was sitting when they introduced him to the third baby."

Casey closed her eyes, still unable to believe the news herself. "How is such a thing even possible? How could we have taken so many ultrasounds without a hint of a third baby?"

Erica shrugged. "Maybe she was playing peekaboo behind her larger brothers. In any event, at least her surprise appearance saved you from worrying about triplets all these months."

Casey squeezed her eyes shut, still trying to fathom that she'd given birth to three children. *Three.* Granted, her body was more than willing to believe such a fact. Despite the glowing reports she'd been given by Erica and the other nurses on her condition, she felt as if she'd been hit by a Mack truck.

Nevertheless, she couldn't deny that she was feeling pretty proud of herself. Proud, exhausted and nervous.

A soft tap at the door caused her to throw a glance at the clock on the wall. Nine o'clock. Since the maternity ward demanded "quiet time" from 10:00 p.m. to 9:00 a.m., there had been no visitors yet. But judging by the sudden thumping of her heart, she knew who waited on the other side of the door.

"How do I look?" she asked quickly, fluffing her hair and pinching her cheeks.

"Radiant," Erica murmured, kissing her cheek.

As Erica moved to open the door, Casey prayed her friend hadn't lied to her. So much had happened since Stephen had proposed and looped the chain holding his ring around her neck.

She touched the ruby as if to draw strength from the glowing jewel. This meeting was going to be awkward—it had to be awkward. Stephen must have spent the night wondering if she'd bent the truth in informing him she was only having twins. Or maybe the reality of three more mouths to feed had become too much to contemplate. Or...

Erica slipped through the door, and Casey gripped the blankets, licking her lips and praying she wouldn't burst into tears if Stephen looked angry or frustrated or...

The door opened and Stephen's dark head moved into view. His hair was tousled and still damp from a recent shower, his jaw freshly shaven. But his eyes were what captured her attention and released her heart from its prison of uncertainty.

"You are amazing," Stephen breathed. Then he stepped into the room, revealing a huge bouquet of flowers, a basket of magazines and assorted candy, and a flat cardboard box.

"Pizza," she said, sighing in wonder.

"Erica said you didn't get much to eat last night and you were dying for something 'noninstitutional.'"

"My hero," she murmured. Then, not knowing how to continue, she looked down at her hands again. His gifts and compliments were encouraging, but she had to know if he'd changed his mind about the marriage, about becoming father to her children. He looked happy—deliriously so. But that didn't mean he still wanted to marry her.

Sensing her change in mood, he quickly set his offerings on the side table. Then, after muttering over the release mechanism on the safety bar to her bed, he nudged her shoulder.

"Move over, woman," he ordered gruffly.

When she didn't move, he gently lifted her, sliding her toward the opposite edge so that he had a sliver of space. Perching next to her, he reached for the chain that hung around her neck.

Her eyes closed in hope, dread, confusion. But when she felt the kiss of the gold band around her finger, her worries drained away, leaving a honey-warm sense of joy in their place.

"I think they'll let you put it on now," he whispered. "As long as you still want me."

She looked up at him then, tears beading her

lashes. There was no denying the love she found shining from his eyes, the adoration, the wonder.

He loved her.

He would always love her.

Just as she would always love him.

"You don't mind that there are three?" she asked hoarsely.

"Mind?" He slid the ring onto her finger, then kissed her palm. "I'm the luckiest man on earth. I have you, six daughters and a pair of sons. What more could anyone ask for?"

"Peace and quiet," she said faintly.

He shook his head, his arms wrapping around her shoulders and drawing her close.

"Two highly overrated commodities," he said, kissing the top of her head. "Granted, we're going to have our hands full—for the rest of our lives, most likely. But I wouldn't have it any other way."

She snuggled against him, the weariness of her body forgotten as she listened to the thump of his heart beneath her ear.

"Really?" she asked one last time.

"Really." His kiss was soft and sweet and full of promise. "You make my life complete."

Epilogue

"You've got quite a crowd, Casey," Erica remarked as she peered through the peephole of the bride's changing room to the chapel beyond.

Casey doubted that the peephole had been an original amenity to the church. But according to Nola Wilkens, the aperture had been in the same place, between the same two ancient bricks, when she'd been married fifty years ago. Legend had it that some enterprising mother had drilled the hole to insure her son-in-law arrived as promised. Then, to cover her crime, she'd donated an elaborate painting depicting the Prodigal Son, and the peephole had never been repaired since.

"Stephen's congregation is a large one," Casey said as she smoothed the gauzy veil over her face. "I bet it will be standing room only by the time they all show up."

"When I mentioned a crowd, I wasn't referring to the good people of Ruckerville," Erica mumbled. "I can see at least…three camera crews from the state television news affiliates, a dozen reporters, and one of the anchors from that Wednesday night news magazine.''

Casey blinked at Erica in disbelief. ''You've got to be kidding.''

''Nope. You're news, honey.''

Casey grimaced. ''They'd better not show up at the reception.''

''Trust me. They'll be there. This is bigger than a Taylor-Burton wedding.''

''Hardly.''

Erica tossed Casey a look that brimmed with laughter. ''Trust me. Stephen mentioned this morning that he's already been approached for several made-for-television movies.''

Casey's jaw dropped. ''Why?''

''You've got everything the public wants to see in one package. Down-home values, romance, babies, sex—''

''We never—''

''You will,'' Erica said slyly.

''You're making this whole story up.''

''It's the truth. Honest. Stephen said one of the offers was in the six-digit range.''

''Before or after the decimal,'' Casey said ruefully as she grasped the train of her heavy satin gown and swept it out of her way as she turned.

''Before.''

It was Erica's reverent tone that finally captured and held Casey's attention.

''You're serious, aren't you?'' Casey breathed.

''Incredibly serious.''

Grasping the bouquet of lilies and roses that

waited on the table, Erica took Casey's lax hand and folded her fingers around the base.

Casey scrambled to make sense of the information she'd just been given. "But we could never take money for…"

"For what? Showing the rest of the world what true romance and commitment means?" Erica asked as she fluffed Casey's cathedral-length veil and eased the train into place behind her.

"But it would be wrong to sell our story," Casey insisted.

"Why?"

"Because…"

Rich strains of organ music floated to them from the chapel.

Erica finished Casey's sentence with a chiding "Because it would be a bad thing to show people how much you love Stephen? How much you both love your children?"

"No, but…"

"But what?" Erica's voice dropped to a whisper. "Six digits, Casey. Don't you see? You told me it was nothing short of a miracle that you, Stephen and the children all found one another. Now that same higher power is providing the means for a few incidentals like shoes, prom dresses, college. You can't refuse. You don't want Stephen's Boss thinking he's ungrateful." Her voice dropped to a whisper. "And by that, I mean The Boss."

With that, Erica pushed open the doors to the foyer, revealing the bridal party that waited to enter the chapel.

As Casey's eyes fell on the quintuplets with their blond curls, white organdy dresses, ruffled socks and pale patent leather shoes, she exhaled, the last of her misgivings seeping away like sand in an hourglass.

She had never doubted that she and Stephen could give their family all the love they needed. But she would have been a fool not to want to give them more. She'd agonized over helping Stephen to provide for their children. But it seemed that providence had taken care of such arrangements, just as Erica had claimed. Their own romance would allow them to save enough money for the future to give their children a good education and a chance to pursue their dreams.

Moving forward, she was suddenly eager for the ceremony to commence. Quickly, she blew each of the children a kiss, then briefly fussed over the three babies ensconced in the old-fashioned wicker pram.

"Thank you for taking care of the children this morning," she said to Stephen's mother.

Katie Dubois's eyes already sparkled with happy tears.

"My pleasure." She sighed, then giggled like a young girl. "When I told Stephen it was up to him to provide me with grandchildren, I had no idea he would be so thorough—and so quick, too. I can hardly wait to spoil them all."

With a final sniff, Katie leaned forward and lifted Casey's veil. "Be happy, my dear."

As the musical prelude reached a crescendo, they all took their places and the double doors opened

wide to reveal a chapel crushed with people and be-
decked with flowers from the rectory's garden.

The audience stood en masse, giving Casey little
more than a glimpse of her bridegroom and the tall
dark priest who stood with him as best man.

"Let the games begin," Erica muttered under her
breath.

As ring bearer, Bert was the first to walk down the
aisle. Next, wearing flowing chiffon gowns, came
Casey's bridesmaids. Myrtle carried a basket of rose
petals that she scattered over the patterned runner—
her new hearing aids planted firmly in place so that
she could hear "every peep."

Then came Anne, looking younger and much more
relaxed than usual. She'd even bought herself a new
pair of shoes, pretty pale pink pumps with very *non-*
orthopedic heels.

Mrs. Dubois waited until the elderly members of
the wedding party were halfway down the aisle, then
proudly rolled the antique pram to her spot on the
first pew. Even Casey could read her enjoyment as
the audience dissolved into ooh's and aah's at the
sight of the month-old triplets.

The girls were next, each one making their way to
the front of the chapel with more decorum and dig-
nity than Casey had ever witnessed in the toddlers.
Briefly, Casey wondered what enticing reward had
been used to bribe them as Erica flashed her a
thumbs-up sign and fell into step, her slim body regal
and beautiful in a dramatic plum-colored sheath.

Then it was Casey's turn.

Her knees were shaking—although she didn't

know why. There was nothing on earth that she would rather do than marry Stephen Dubois, to become his helpmate at the rectory, the mother of his children, the love of his life.

As if sensing her thoughts, Stephen stepped forward so that he could see her through the crowd. Instantly, Casey's nervousness dissipated and she knew that all she'd needed to continue was the sight of his smile.

Taking his outstretched hand, she joined him, standing serenely at his side as they took their place in front of the altar. Vainly, she tried to gather details to last a lifetime, but the ceremony rushed past her with incredible speed until, finally, Stephen lifted her veil and kissed her. Not just as a man who adored her.

But as her husband.

Her heart mate.

Turning, they basked in the delight and approval of all present. Then in a hailstorm of rice, they hurried down the aisle and onto the church steps for pictures and the flood of guests who wished to congratulate them.

In the gardens where the reception would take place, a small band began to play. Within minutes, Casey saw Bert and Anne shepherding the quintuplets onto the grass, where the girls erupted into squeals and chased one another in circles.

Mrs. Dubois joined Stephen's brother, Jean-Luc, in the shade of a massive oak, and was soon holding court with the babies. Erica was already being besieged by men, and Myrtle—who could finally hear the conversations around her—was directing the catering staff like a drill sergeant. In the distant parking lot, Casey even caught sight of her divorced mothers group decorating their "getaway van"—complete with its eight car seats—with toilet paper and shaving cream.

"It's perfect, isn't it?" Stephen said next to her ear.

She squeezed his hand. "Absolutely perfect."

"Pastor and Mrs. Dubois!" someone called, and they somehow managed to tear their gazes apart to discover that a battery of reporters and camera crews had formed on the steps in front of them. "How does it feel to be married?"

Stephen lifted Casey's hand and kissed it. "Fantastic!"

"And do you think your new marriage can survive the demands of so many children?"

Stephen looked at Casey and they both grinned conspiratorially. At the same time, they said, "The Dubois family has more than enough love to go around."

Then Stephen wrapped an arm around Casey's waist and drew her down the steps, expertly steering his way through the gaggle of reporters. "We'll answer all the questions you want to ask. Later. Right now, we need to lead the first waltz so people can dance. Then we have a cake to cut. Why don't you join us?"

Casey laughed at the adept way Stephen side-stepped a minicam, then twirled her toward the platform of planks that served as a makeshift dance floor.

"Just one more question!" a woman called, her pen poised above her notebook. "Do the two of you plan on having any more children?"

Stephen and Casey froze in their tracks, glanced up at each other, then grinned. Before they could answer, Jean-Luc called from under the tree, "For heaven's sake, don't give them any ideas!"

The reporters laughed and the moment was over. One by one, the cameramen and journalists drifted toward the refreshments, and the guests to the dance floor, while the children gravitated toward the quintuplets.

"Well?" Stephen asked when no one seemed to be paying attention to them any longer. "What are your views on more children?"

Casey's heart thumped in her chest. But when she caught Stephen's wicked grin, she knew he was only teasing. They had plenty of time before such earth-shattering decisions would have to be broached. A very, *very* long time.

"I wouldn't be opposed to more," she said after pondering the idea. "But I wouldn't be opposed to enjoying the ones we already have, either."

He grinned in approval. "I knew there was a reason why I married you."

"After all, we could always move from my Queen Anne back to the rectory if needed," Casey continued. "We could fill up the whole dormitory someday."

She thought she saw the color ebb from Stephen's cheeks ever so faintly.

"Bite your tongue," he finally muttered.

Casey laughed, snuggling against him, reveling in the strength of his arms and the heady sexual energy that reminded her that finally—*finally* they would be making love.

"You wouldn't like a dormitory full of kids?" she asked, tongue in cheek.

Stephen's dark eyes sparkled with wickedness—an expression she never would have thought possible in a pastor.

"That depends," he murmured, bending to speak next to her ear. "I'll consider the idea..." he whispered, then nipped her ear in a way that sent a jolt of passion streaking through her system.

Her knees threatened to give way entirely, when his tongue touched the same spot so recently afflicted by his teeth.

"You'll consider the idea?" she repeated, more to keep herself from dissolving with desire than any real desire to hear the answer.

"Mmm. As long as we go about helping Mother Nature deliver any future Dubois children in the traditional manner—you and me...together...making love."

"Amen to that," she breathed, pulling him down for a kiss. "Amen to that...."

COMING NEXT MONTH

#785 THE LAST STUBBORN COWBOY by Judy Christenberry
4 Tots for 4 Texans
With his friends married and in a family way, Mac Gibbons thought the bet was over, and he was safe from the matchmaking moms of Cactus, Texas. That is, until he stopped to help a lady in distress and looked down into the blue eyes of new doc Samantha Collins...and her baby daughter. A daughter who looked amazingly just like Mac!

#786 RSVP...BABY by Pamela Browning
The Wedding Party
The last thing Bianca D'Alessandro needed was to be a bridesmaid at a family wedding. Especially since she'd be bringing a pint-size guest no one knew about. She could pass off the whispers, but she couldn't avoid the best man, Neill Bellamy—the father of her secret baby....

#787 THE OVERNIGHT GROOM by Elizabeth Sinclair
Oops! Still Married!
Grant Waverly's career was his mistress...until he found out he was married! Kathleen Donovan had been his one true love—and apparently his wife for the past seven years, though neither one knew it. But now that Grant had a wife, he intended to keep her!

#788 DEPUTY DADDY by Charlotte Maclay
Lawman Johnny Fuentes didn't know what to do with the beautiful but very pregnant woman with amnesia who was found wandering in town—except take her home. Trouble was, soon she began believing he was her husband!

Look us up on-line at: http://www.romance.net